DEATH IN AN ELEGANT CITY

DEATH IN AN ELEGANT CITY

BOOK FOUR IN THE MURDER ON LOCATION SERIES

SARA ROSETT

DEATH IN AN ELEGANT CITY
Book Four in the *Murder on Location* series
An English Village Murder Mystery
Published by McGuffin Ink

Second Paperback Edition: October 2016
First Paperback Edition: April 2016
ISBN: 978-0-9982535-3-4
Cover Design: James at GoOnWrite.com

❀ Created with Vellum

ABOUT DEATH IN AN ELEGANT CITY

Sightseeing can be murder...

Location scout Kate Sharp is thrilled to be part of a scouting trip to the historic city of Bath, England to research the location for a Jane Austen documentary. But before Kate gets a chance to stroll the elegant boulevards where Austen once lived, murder cuts the sightseeing short. Now Kate must rearrange her itinerary and find the killer before she and the production are shut down permanently.

Perfect for fans of British detective mysteries, Death in an Elegant City *blends the puzzle of a whodunit with the mystique of Jane Austen. It is the fourth installment in the popular* Murder on Location *series, a collection of traditional British cozy mysteries.*

"Evil to some is always good to others."
—Jane Austen, *Emma*

CHAPTER 1

THE TRIP DIDN'T START WELL.

It should have been a short, easy drive from Nether Woodsmoor in Derbyshire to Bath in Somerset. It wasn't far in miles—only about a four-hour drive when you begin at three in the morning—but the tension inside the van was palpable, and I was already dreading the next three days of non-stop togetherness that our location scouting trip required.

I had been able to tune out the almost constant sniping in the van, managing to snatch a few hours sleep, but Elise DuPont's strident tone had carried from the driver's seat to the back row, jerking me out of my drowsy state. I saw the outline of a city glowing in the distant darkness and checked the time. Almost six, so it had to be Bath.

Alex stirred beside me on the bench seat and straightened. Catching a glimpse of a sign that stated Bath was only a few kilometers away, he muttered, "Thank goodness," and stretched his arm along the back of the seat, casually wrapping my shoulders. He glanced toward the front of the van. "Despite the atmosphere, it's good to be together again," he said, in his relaxed, easy way.

I found myself smiling back at him. "Yes, it is," I said and wondered why I'd been so worried about seeing Alex again face-to-face.

The last few months had been a little rough for our burgeoning relationship. The Jane Austen documentary production that we worked for had completed its first three episodes and gone on hiatus in June. With no guarantee that more episodes would be ordered, both Alex and I had looked for new location scouting jobs. Alex had landed a job working on a fantasy film, which had taken him to Croatia for two months during the summer in July and August. I was a temporary transplanted American and didn't want my time in England to be over, so I'd stayed in the little village of Nether Woodsmoor and managed to pick up a few location scouting jobs in the surrounding area, one of which was for a BBC crime drama that filmed two episodes in Derbyshire, but the work petered out after that.

I was barely scraping by, doing occasional scouting for a couple of print ads when my hypochondriac mother, who lived in the States, had actually become ill, an event that shocked both of us. I moved out of Honeysuckle Cottage, which had been my snug and cozy home for several months, and returned to Southern California to take care of her.

She had made a full, but slow, recovery from a serious bout with pneumonia. Even on her worst days she tried to engineer meetings between me and any male medical professional who had the misfortune to be assigned to her case. While she had once thought only doctors were worth consideration in the matrimonial stakes, she had now broadened her view to include respiratory therapists, hospital administrators, and male nurses.

Once I was sure mom was out of danger, I'd taken some location scouting jobs that old friends had thrown my way, adding a couple of print ads as well as a music video to my resume. When the news came that the Jane Austen documentary production had been renewed for three more episodes, I immediately booked an airline ticket, despite knowing that the logical thing to do would be to stay in California, which had more job opportunities.

On the personal side, I enjoyed being with Alex, but we were so different—he was relaxed, easy-going, and had an effortless charm that drew people to him. I, on the other hand, was a *tad* more structured and analytical, which meant that the whole time we were apart I was running through the possible outcomes of our relationship and kept coming back to the inescapable conclusion that we were too different to work as a couple. But despite all the logical misgivings I had about our relationship, when the news came about the new episodes my heart overruled my mind, and I'd raided my savings account. I had just enough to cover the airfare to escape the smoggy dry heat of California and return to cool, green England and pre-production.

Alex and I had done our best to stay in touch during the months apart, but any separation takes its toll, and after four months of echoey phone calls and fuzzy video chats, everything felt slightly awkward. We'd only been back on the same continent for a few days, and I'd decided it was too much to expect that we would be perfectly comfortable with each other right away. Things were definitely different. We weren't quite where we had been in the spring. Our easy camaraderie had faded a bit, and things felt slightly strained, but snuggled into the curve of Alex's arm felt like exactly the right place to be.

A deep voice from the front of the van drew my attention back to the present. "We can easily work in a couple of references to *Pride and Prejudice* and *Sense and Sensibility*," said Cyrus Blakely, the production's newly assigned director, whose deep tone and crisp aristocratic accent conveyed exasperation. The headlights of a passing car flickered over the inside of the van, momentarily lighting the longish golden hair that he combed straight back from his high forehead. With his fine flyaway hair floating around his face and his large brown eyes, he reminded me of a lion. He had a King of the Beasts attitude to match the look, and had spent the first moments of the early-morning hours strutting around the van, informing us where we would sit, how to load the luggage, and which route to take.

I wasn't a huge fan of our producer, Elise—we'd gotten off on the wrong foot initially, but had now settled into a truce—but I couldn't help feeling a bit sorry for her. Apparently, the backers of the documentary wanted Cyrus attached to the project, and Elise had little say in the decision…or at least that was the rumor that my friend Melissa had heard. And she usually had all the info about that sort of thing.

"Still arguing," Alex marveled, his American accent contrasting with the clipped British voices coming from the front of the van. Like me, Alex was an American, although he had lived all around the world while growing up because of his father's diplomatic job.

"I know," I said quietly. "I thought they would run out of steam by Birmingham."

Elise didn't reply to Cyrus's comment about *Pride and Prejudice*. Instead, she kept her gaze on the road and gave a sharp shake of her head, which dislodged another strand of her streaky gray-blond hair from her bun. Elise wasn't one of those women who worried about her appearance. She was the lowest maintenance woman I'd ever met. She wore black every day, but not because it was chic. She'd told me once that a single color meant she didn't have to fuss about wardrobe choices. Today she had on a cavernous black cape with black jeans and black ankle boots. Each day her saggy bun was held in place with whatever skewer-like implement was handy. Today it looked like a drinking straw was doing the job.

"We've been over this ground before, Cyrus," Elise said in an accent just as posh as Cyrus's. "The documentary has already covered *Pride and Prejudice* and *Sense and Sensibility*. Jane Austen wrote more than two books during her lifetime, and we are documenting her *entire* life."

We had wound our way through the more modern outskirts of Bath to the center of the city. I tried to ignore the bickering at the front of the van as I took in the elegant boulevards lined with buildings of the golden-hued local limestone, but the van was such a confined space that I couldn't escape hearing the argument.

Cyrus shifted and his seat creaked, his every move

conveying annoyance. "Viewers like Elizabeth and Darcy and—"

"Which we delved into," Elise said, sharply. "In fact, we delved into it so deeply that I don't see how we could find anything else to say about them."

I heard a snuffling noise and glanced at the row in front of Alex and me. Felix, our cinematographer, started and jerked awake. He rubbed his hand across his face and struggled to a more upright position. Felix usually had the sartorial splendor of a crumpled piece of paper, but with the travel and the early start, he now looked like a crumpled piece of paper that had been run over a few times... and left in the rain.

"Still at it, are they?" he asked. I sent Felix a quelling glance. He wasn't exactly diplomatic. In fact, he seemed to thrive on conflict, almost enjoying it. I was glad he'd slept almost the entire drive. Who knows what state Cyrus and Elise would be in if Felix had been goading them on for hours.

But Elise had heard Felix's comment. "No, it's settled," she said in an imperious voice. "Cyrus must get it through his head." She glanced quickly over her shoulder to look at Felix, then she gave Cyrus, who was seated on the first bench seat, a significant look before refocusing on the road. "The subject is closed. There are plenty of Jane Austen-related sites to explore in Bath and none of them have anything to do with either of those books. Paul, show him the spreadsheet," Elise commanded, and Paul's lanky form shifted in the front passenger seat.

Paul was the production's first assistant director, or A.D., as he was called for short. He always had a pencil stuck behind his left ear, and he was usually a whirlwind of action and motion. But he'd been so still and quiet that I'd forgotten he was in the van. He reached out a boney Ichabod Crane-like arm and held out a computer tablet toward Cyrus, but Cyrus waved it away with a sniff.

"I never touch those things, my lad. That's why I have you around."

"You made sure of that, didn't you?" Paul said in a tone so bitter it drew my attention away from the view. I didn't know Paul all that well. He was constantly on the go, but he was always a soothing presence compared to Elise's acerbic personality. I'd never heard him use a tone like that. Now that I thought about it, he'd also been subdued this morning when we loaded the van. I'd assumed it was the early hour, but as Paul glanced back, I noticed that he looked...angry, I realized. Cyrus didn't notice Paul's hostile look.

"Just one big happy family, aren't we?" Felix muttered, his voice pitched low so that it didn't carry to the front of the van. He stretched, and his already half untucked dress shirt pulled out of the waistband of his pants. "Yep, *Northanger Abbey* and *Persuasion*—now there's a recipe for cancellation, if I ever heard one," he said slightly louder.

He ignored the searing glance that Elise directed at him through the rearview mirror and turned his profile with his prominent brow to the window. I watched Felix for a second, wondering briefly what had happened to make him such a curmudgeon. He was only in his thirties—possibly late thirties—but had the grumpy disposition of a set-in-his-ways elderly man.

It must be the early start. It had put us all in a bad

mood, I decided, determinedly suppressing the uneasy feeling. The odd hours and extended time spent together on a scouting trip usually brought on a sort of giddy *esprit de corps,* which, granted, was often brought on by the enforced togetherness and lack of sleep, but still…this trip felt nothing like that. There were too many bad vibes.

We had reached the central area of Bath, and Elise expertly spun the steering wheel, guiding the van into a parallel parking slot beside a rusticated stone wall over seven feet tall. A substantial stone balustrade ran atop the wall, high overhead.

Elise threw the van into "park," climbed out, and stalked across the street to a smaller road, a pedestrian walkway, that branched off the road perpendicularly. The cobblestone street she walked along was lined with shops, hotels, and restaurants, all with neoclassical façades. Elise went to the white doorway with a beautiful fanlight glowing brightly. A brass plaque by the door read, "Bath Spa Hotel."

The rest of us climbed out of the van more slowly. After the warmth of the van, the chilly November air was bracing. I fastened the top button on my peacoat. Felix surveyed the dark street, hands in his pockets, then he doubtfully studied the hotel. "Doesn't look like it will have a bar."

Cyrus, his sport coat flapping as he moved quickly around the van, threw open the back doors. "I've known Dominic and Annie Bell for years." The wind whipped his long hair around, causing it to stand on end. "I always stay with them when I'm in town. Excellent hotel. One of the finest boutique hotels in Bath."

I scanned the street we'd parked on, then took a few steps toward an open paved courtyard that began where the high stone wall ended. The towering Gothic spires of a church were visible against the sky, which was slowly brightening, transitioning from black to navy. "That must be Bath Abbey," I said, taking in the flying buttresses, the pointed arch windows, and the rose window at the front of the church.

Alex looked at me critically. "We better get you some coffee."

I threw him a grin. I was not at my best in the morning, especially before coffee. "I mean, *obviously* that's the Abbey…so…" I swiveled slightly, looking back at the high stone wall, "those must be the Roman Baths behind the wall."

I'd used the time on my long flight back to England to prep for the scouting trip, reading guidebooks and paying special attention to the areas Jane Austen had frequented as well as the locations she'd used in her books. The Roman Baths and the more modern Pump Room figured prominently in both her life and her writing.

"Indeed it is," Cyrus said as I removed my camera from its case and snapped a few quick shots of the Abbey. I didn't have to get my camera out of my luggage because I almost always carried it with me, something I'd picked up from my first boss when I was learning the ropes of location scouting.

"Brilliant location," Cyrus said. "Can't be beat. Ah, here is Dominic, the proprietor."

A tall, broad-shouldered man came out of the hotel's open doorway, temporarily blocking the light. He trotted down the steps and hurried across the street with a long stride to greet Cyrus and take his suitcase.

A petite woman with curly ginger-colored hair followed him out, but remained on the hotel's top step leaning on a pair of crutches. Her right leg was in a cast from her knee to her foot.

"And here's Annie," Cyrus announced in ringing tones. My friend Melissa had told me Cyrus had started his career as an actor, then later switched to directing. I believed her. His voice would have carried to the back row of any theater and he had probably woken any still-sleeping residents farther along the street.

I took a final shot of the Abbey then reached for my suitcase, but Alex beat me to the suitcase handle.

"Allow me," he said, and I gladly stepped back. Lugging equipment was one of the downsides of scouting trips.

We crossed to the open doorway where everyone had stopped.

"Annie, darling, what happened?" Cyrus asked as he planted a quick kiss on Annie's cheek, then stepped back and gestured at the crutches.

"I'm an idiot, is what happened. Tripped on the basement stairs, and now I have to pay for it. Weeks with this thing," she lifted a crutch and shook it at Cyrus. "A terrible fate for someone who hates to slow down."

"A terrible fate for all of us," Dominic amended in his deep voice, and Annie rolled her eyes at him.

"Come in, all of you." She tucked the crutch under her arm and turned with an economy of motion and swiftness that made it clear she had mastered the use of her crutches.

The bright light of the entry highlighted Annie's ginger-colored curls as she said, "Welcome to Bath Spa Hotel. You'll have the whole place to yourself for the next few days. Please let us know if you need anything at all."

The wainscoted entry was quite small. Annie thumped her way over to an interior door that separated a tiny office from the entry area. A window had been cut into the wall that separated the office from the reception area and I could see a desk and filing cabinet through the opening. Annie put her crutches aside and deftly switched places with Dominic, who had been collecting keys from a row of pigeonholes behind the desk. Annie hopped on her good foot and took a seat behind the desk. She waved a hand toward the adjoining room. "Breakfast service begins at seven in the dining room, which is beyond the parlor there, and we can help you book a table at a restaurant or a tour, but it sounds as if you'll be quite busy."

Because the entry was so crowded, Alex and I stepped into the connecting room. The parlor was more spacious with bow windows that overlooked the cobblestoned street. Club chairs and small tables were scattered around the room. A kitchen was the next room on the ground floor, and beyond it, I could see women moving around a dining room, setting up for breakfast. The rich smell of coffee permeated the air, and my mouth watered.

Cyrus tapped Felix on the shoulder and pointed to the back of the parlor where a small wooden bar filled one corner beside a door to what looked like a courtyard garden. "There's your bar," Cyrus said as he finger-combed his hair that had been tossed around by the wind off his high forehead. "What did I tell you? Everything you need. And we all know you need a bar to be fully functioning."

Felix looked perturbed at this statement. Cyrus's tone was joking, but there was something else there, too, a cutting, almost malicious undercurrent as well. Felix was a grouch, but I'd never known him to have any sort of problem with alcohol, which seemed to be what Cyrus was insinuating. I glanced at Alex, and he lifted a shoulder, his expression conveying that he didn't know what Cyrus was trying to say either.

Dominic handed the bundle of keys to Elise, who had also moved into the parlor area where she was consulting with Paul. Paul had his ever-present clipboard balanced on his computer tablet. He took the pencil from behind his ear and checked off room numbers as Elise distributed keys. "Cyrus," she said, "you're by yourself in Room Two. I have Room One. Paul, you're in the single, Room Four. Alex, you and Felix have Room Three. Kate, you're in Room Five, with Melissa—whenever she shows up," Elise finished, her tone indicating that Melissa might never arrive.

"She's already here in Bath," I said. "She texted me yesterday. The Fashion Museum wanted them to begin setting up yesterday." Melissa had worked in Continuity during the first three episodes we'd filmed, but she was interested in fashion and wanted to move to Costuming. Her personal wardrobe was inventive and quirky, and I'd told her shifting over to Costume was a perfect fit for her. She'd rolled her eyes at my pun, but said that she felt more in her element than she ever had in Continuity.

When Elise mentioned that she had a contact at the Fashion Museum in Bath who was interested in running a special exhibit related to the Jane Austen documentary,

Melissa had jumped at the opportunity to be a liaison between the Fashion Museum and Parkview Hall, a stately home that was one of our go-to shooting locations for the documentary. Parkview Hall had an extensive range of period clothing tucked away in their storerooms, some of which they had kindly let us borrow when we'd filmed several scenes depicting Regency life on location there. They were just as generous to the Fashion Museum, lending them several examples of Regency attire for the exhibit. I didn't expect to see much of Melissa since the preview party for the exhibit was scheduled for Saturday evening, only two days away.

"Good," Elise said shortly then looked at Paul. "Get in touch with Melissa. See if everything is on-track. We'll need to go there, probably tomorrow, and see if we can use the exhibit for a Jane in the Modern World feature."

Paul nodded, switching to his computer tablet.

Elise turned to speak to the group. "Drop your bags in your rooms and meet me back here in ten minutes."

Dominic's large figure moved through the parlor to the area that opened to the kitchen. He clasped his hands together. "Before you scatter, a few things...we are a Grade II historic building, so that means we haven't been able to install an elevator. Insert groans here," he said with a smile. "However, Annie and I—"

"You mean Mia," Annie called out from the reception area as she waved her crutch and used it to point to a young woman in her late teens who appeared from the kitchen. Mia wore an apron over a polo shirt with the hotel's name embroidered on it. Her thick chestnut bangs ended just above her bright green eyes. The rest of her long hair was pulled back into a ponytail, except for two curling tendrils that framed her dimpled smile.

"I'm staying put right here with my book," Annie said, gesturing to a paperback copy of *Northanger Abbey* that rested on the ledge of the office window. "I'm getting quite a lot of reading for my book club done lately," Annie said ruefully.

"Right. *Mia* and I," Dominic said, "are happy to carry your bags to your rooms. Just a couple of things before we do that. Here is your code for the night latch." He handed out slips of paper to all of us with a short string of numbers. "Use that to get in, if you'll be out after eleven. That way, Annie and I don't have to wait up for you until the small hours of the morning. You're free to party until dawn, if you like. Dining room, here." He gestured behind him. "Bar in the back. WC down those stairs there in the basement."

He pointed to a set of iron circular stairs in a corner of the parlor. "If you have extra bags or equipment, we can store it in our storage room down there." He paused, glancing around our group. "No takers on that? Right, then. Let's begin the climb." He picked up Elise's bag and moved through a kitchen area with two counters, a sink, and an impressive-looking cappuccino machine to another set of narrow circular steps. "We had to make the most of every bit of space," he said over his shoulder, "so the path to the rooms takes you through the kitchen. We only serve breakfast and have quite a few locals who stop in for breakfast or coffee, but after about ten we won't be in your way too much." The staircase he trotted up was wooden and carpeted.

Mia snatched up my bag and said, "Room Five?"

"Yes, but I can carry that."

"Oh, no worries. I do it all the time." And she must have, because she skimmed up the tapering circular steps quickly to the top floor. Along the way, we passed Cyrus and Elise, who had stopped at their separate rooms on the first floor above the ground floor. We also left Alex, Felix, and Paul behind on the next floor. One more twist of the staircase brought Mia and me to the top of the building and Room Five.

After stooping over to reach the keyhole set low in the door, Mia set my suitcase down at the foot of one of the two single beds. A bright wallpaper of butterflies filled one wall. It was so dazzling and busy that it was hard to look away from it, but I managed to scan the rest of the room.

A dressing table stood in one corner and a small window seat completed the room's decor. There wasn't room for anything else. I'd read enough Regency literature to know that the sloping ceiling meant that this was a former servant's room.

"The loo is through here," Mia said, pointing to a door with a raised step, which opened into a tiny bathroom. "Oh, and I'm to remind you that there isn't a safe in the rooms, but if you have something valuable—watches, jewelry, something like that," she said, her gaze darting from my wrist to my earlobes to my tiny, rather beat-up suitcase, "Dominic will put it in the vault downstairs...if you have anything," she finished uncertainly. "Perhaps your camera? It does look expensive."

I'd forgotten I had slipped the camera strap around my neck. I used my camera so often that it was almost a part of me. "It is, but I'll keep it with me." I stepped to the side so she could get by me to leave the room.

She paused on the landing. "I know it's the smallest room and at the top of the stairs," she said in a conspiratorial whisper, "but it's also the quietest because it's at the back of the house...less street noise. And at this time of the year, no worries about it being too hot." She smiled, deepening her dimples before clattering down the stairs.

I closed the door and went to kneel on the window seat, pulling back the shutters from the window. I peered down to the small square of concrete that must be the courtyard garden, but my stomach fluttered, and I transferred my gaze to the rooftops. I couldn't see much of Bath—mostly other rooftops, but it was Bath, a part of England I'd never explored. The sun was higher now, spreading a golden light across the city, and I wanted to get out there.

I tucked my room key and a map of the city into my tote bag, checked that I had some spare batteries for the camera, an extra memory card, and my Moleskine notebook, then stepped into the hall. Feeling a bit like *Alice in Wonderland,* I stooped over and locked the door with the real key—no key cards at a Grade II listed building, apparently—then headed for the stairs and a cup of coffee.

CHAPTER 2

I TOOK THE STAIRS A bit slower than Mia. The steps were quite narrow, and I wasn't as surefooted as she was. The foot of the stairs opened into the kitchen area where Dominic, Annie, and Mia were working. I crossed through the kitchen and was the last to arrive back in the parlor. Elise hadn't waited for me. A few locals had arrived, and Mia was busy at the cappuccino machine. I heard the clink of silverware from the dining room and wanted to slip in there to search for coffee, but Elise was already speaking.

"We need to get started straightaway. The weather forecast is not good. It's supposed to cloud over and rain this afternoon. We'll split up so we can cover as much ground as possible."

Alex stood on the outskirts of the group. He tilted his hand away from his leg as I approached, and I slipped my hand into his.

Elise said, "Felix, I need you to take a look at Pulteney Bridge and the river, see if it would be feasible to shoot there." Elise consulted her list. "Alex, you have the northern area, the Crescent and the Circus. Get exterior shots while the light is good. If you have time, also go by the Assembly Rooms."

Elise glanced down at our linked hands as she said, "Kate you have the central area, the Abbey, the old town square bit, and the Roman Baths. Again, concentrate on exteriors while the light is good, but get some interior shots of the Baths as well."

I nodded and gave Alex's hand a squeeze before pulling away. Elise seemed to delight in separating us. Since we'd become a couple, she rarely assigned us to the same task. Maybe she was afraid that we wouldn't get anything done if we worked together, but Alex and I were professionals. We always got our work done, and it wouldn't be different if we worked together—if she'd give us a chance. But it didn't appear that we'd get that opportunity this morning.

Elise folded the piece of paper she'd been reading from and turned to Cyrus. "You'll come with Paul and me to the meeting with the mayor's office, then we'll check the pedestrian walkways…although I don't have much hope of being able to shoot anything historical. Too many modern street lamps and red telephone boxes—which have been converted to wifi points," she added with an exasperated shake of her head. "But they might work for a feature or a backdrop for an interview. We need a meeting point. Let's see, the Pump Room is fairly central. Meet there at noon. Paul, Cyrus, let's get going."

Cyrus, who had been lounging in a club chair at the back of the parlor near the bar, stood. "I won't be joining you for the meeting with the city's illustrious mayor."

"Of course you will," Elise said as she flung her black wool cape around her shoulders and worked her fingers into black knit gloves. The early November day was slated to be cold with the temperature only about ten degrees above freezing.

"No, I won't." Cyrus's tone was firm.

Elise, who had turned toward the door, slowly rotated back to face him. "You need to be there. You're the director. You're Cyrus Blakely. That's the reason the backers insisted you be part of the project. You have a cachet," she said with a sneer. "The mayor and his people will be much more amiable to working with the great Cyrus Blakely. You're coming, and you're going to be charming so that we will be able to get whatever permits and permissions we need."

Cyrus shook his head. "No. I don't work that way. I need to get out and," he waved his hand in a circular motion, "absorb the atmosphere. Soak in the place. It's part of my process. Paperwork is not. That's your area."

"You can't just go out on your own. We have a schedule to keep. Appointments. You *must* be there."

"I'm sure you'll handle everything beautifully."

"You—you are..." Elise sputtered, "insufferable. I cannot believe I have to put up with this. You are simply being difficult and...and contrary. I won't stand for it. You *must* come to the meeting."

"Or what? Would you care to contact Gerald and discuss it with him?" Cyrus transferred his gaze to the ceiling. "I seem to remember a conversation in which Gerald clearly said I was free to do as I liked."

A pink shade had suffused Elise's face, and she had been leaning forward, clearly ready to make her next point, but at the name "Gerald" she drew back. Her chest rose and fell as she breathed through her nose for a few seconds. "Very well. Have it your way," she snapped. "When things fall apart because we can't film where you'd like, the blame will be on you."

She whirled toward the door, the fringe on the cape flying, muttering about disasters and Cyrus's head. Paul slipped out behind her. I didn't envy him, having to bear the brunt of Elise's anger.

A moment of uncomfortable silence filled the little parlor, then Felix, who looked a little less disheveled with his hair combed and shirt tucked in, put two fingers at his temple and saluted Cyrus. "Impressive. Not many people get their own way with Elise." Felix buttoned his coat and wrapped a scarf around his neck. It was looped unevenly and had one short end that only came to his collarbone while the other end dangled down his back to almost his waistline. "Well, friends, I am not so brave as our director. I'm off to meekly complete my commission. To Pulteney Bridge." He crammed a newsboy hat on his head and exited, pausing to hold the door open for Annie, who was now bundled into a coat. She crossed the room quickly, her crutch swinging, and called out to Dominic that she was off to the market. Dominic popped his head out of the kitchen area and said that they needed more oranges. The aroma of sausage and bacon had filled the air and my stomach growled.

"Too bad we can't stay for breakfast," I said to Alex, "but if Elise found out..." I shuddered.

"No," Alex agreed. "That wouldn't be good. But she couldn't object to a cup of coffee."

"Excellent idea. We better get it on the way, though, not here," I said, thinking that if Elise had to double back to the hotel for any reason and found us lingering over a cup of coffee she wouldn't be happy. She was already in a bad mood. I wasn't about to take the chance of making it worse, despite the tempting aroma of coffee wafting out of the dining room.

"Agreed," Alex said then patted his pocket and checked his camera case. "I left my phone upstairs. Let me get it."

He climbed the wooden circular staircase two steps at a time.

Cyrus, who was pouring himself a cup of tea from a pot that had been placed on one of the tables in the parlor along with sugar and cream, said, "Kate, I was sorry to hear about your mother. Distressing for you, I'm sure. So devoted of you to return to the States and nurse her back to health."

"She needed me." I frowned at him. While the words themselves were nice, his tone was disdainful and his glance was knowing.

"I'm sure she did," he said. "The...ah—issue—she has to deal with is...difficult."

"Yes, pneumonia can be scary."

He raised one eyebrow. "That's what they're calling it these days, pneumonia?"

"What are you talking about?" I asked. "She was hospitalized for several weeks."

Cyrus stirred his tea, then put it down on a nearby table. He stepped closer and wrapped one hand across his stomach, then propped his elbow on his arm, and put his index finger over his lips. He spoke quickly, his finger still on his lips. "Let's just say that I know the truth about your history and your mother's unfortunate...struggle."

I knew in an instant what he was insinuating, and I felt a hazy mist of anger sweep over me. My mother had struggled with an addiction to pain medicine, but that had been years ago, and she hadn't had a relapse.

"I don't know where you get your information, Mr. Blakely, but it couldn't be more wrong. My mother was sick...and not in the way you mean."

"Ah, but she has had...problems, shall we say...in the past. I wasn't sure, but now I know. Your reaction confirms it." He smiled and unfolded his arms.

I clenched my hands into fists, then shoved them in my coat pockets. *Do not hit the director,* I mentally chanted.

Cyrus picked up his tea and said casually, "I only want you to know that I'm familiar with your background. Backgrounds are a hobby of mine. Some people collect antiques or cars or salt shakers. I've found people's histories—particularly their secrets—much more interesting."

The intellectual, cooler-headed part of me, which was divorced from the anger that was fizzing through me, realized that I couldn't respond as I wanted to. He wanted to get a rise out of me. I burrowed my hands deeper in my pockets. "What an unrewarding pastime."

"Of course," he continued as if I hadn't spoken, "it would be a shame if you had to run off to the States unexpectedly. I'm sure when you were ready to return there wouldn't be room for you in the production, if that should happen." He sipped from his cup. "So important to know exactly where one stands, isn't it? Then there are no questions, should anything...arise."

"Kate?"

I turned and realized Alex was standing beside me. I had been so focused on Cyrus that I hadn't heard him approach. Alex took one look at my face and said, "We have to be going."

"Fine, yes. Good," Cyrus murmured as he consulted a menu card tucked between a small flower vase and a set of salt and pepper shakers. "I believe I'll have the full English breakfast before I embark on my tour of Bath," he said.

Alex put an arm around my shoulders and steered me out the door. "Let's walk."

"Good idea," I said, and we turned onto the main pedestrian walkway. I set a quick pace. After a few minutes I'd walked off my fury and came back to my surroundings enough to realize that the wind was cold on my cheeks. I slowed. "I think I need that coffee now."

"Let's go over there." Alex nodded to a corner café. I got a table while Alex placed the order. He returned with two large mugs of coffee and a plate with two oversized blueberry muffins.

He set them down and took a seat. "What happened?"

"I discovered that Cyrus is a manipulative, mean person."

I recounted what Cyrus had said, and Alex shook his head. "One look at your face, and I knew it was bad," Alex said. "I have heard rumors about Cyrus…nothing specific, only that people have vowed never to work with him again or left productions he's been involved in."

"It doesn't bode well for the rest of this production." I broke the muffin in half and jelly oozed out of the center. I gobbled a bite before continuing, "That comment he threw at Felix about the bar—it was the same thing, either a taunt to see if he could get a reaction from Felix or a warning that he knew something that Felix would rather the rest of us didn't know. And he's certainly not going out of his way to make things easy with Elise."

"Cyrus seems to have got on the wrong side of everyone within a few hours—even Paul."

"You noticed that, too, in the van?"

Alex nodded. "No idea what happened, but Paul isn't one to act like that."

"He's certainly not." I brushed crumbs from my fingers. "At least we're all on our own this morning. I better get back to the Abbey and the Baths."

"No full English breakfast for us," Alex said as he gathered up the muffin wrappers.

"It was delicious. Just what I needed."

As we left the café I bumped into a young woman on her way inside. I stepped aside, but she stopped in her tracks, her gaze fastened on Alex.

"Alex?" Her head was tilted to one side and her forehead was wrinkled into a frown.

Alex had been holding the door for me, but at his name he focused on the woman. "Viv!"

"It *is* you," she said and surged toward Alex, embracing him quickly. She stepped back, brushing the trailing strands of her reddish-brown hair out of her face. Most of her hair was caught back in a loose braid that fell to her shoulder blades. She had a round face with an upturned nose. She wore no makeup, not even lipstick, and had a fresh-faced, earthy beauty. She wore jeans with rips in the knees and a black tank top under a plaid shirt and a vest lined with sheepskin. Leather bracelets wrapped her wrist and several silver rings encased most of her fingers, even her thumbs. A bike helmet dangled from one hand. "I thought it was you," she said, her face lighting up with delight. "You've hardly changed."

Another customer came to the door that we were blocking, and we all stepped out of the doorway and paused on the sidewalk. Alex touched my shoulder. "Kate this is Viv. I knew her back in my snowboarding days. Viv, this is Kate, my colleague and girlfriend."

Viv widened her blue eyes. "Colleague *and* girlfriend. Impressive. I was dying to fill that girlfriend slot, but Alex wasn't interested," she said with a quick smile, aimed at him.

Her frankness was disarming. When she'd wrapped Alex in a hug, my reaction had been an instinctive urge to tell her to back off, but my initial feeling of territorial protectiveness fell away as I looked at her open face.

Her gaze swept over me. "I can see why I was out of the running for girlfriend—I'm not nearly polished enough," she said, pulling a face as she tugged at her worn jeans.

I'd thought my white knit top and black jeans tucked into my calf-high brown boots with my peacoat was a casual look, but compared to Viv, I did look dressed up. Before I could make some self-deprecating remark, Viv pointed at the cameras that both Alex and I sported. "Here in Bath for some sightseeing, are you?"

"No, Kate and I are location scouts."

Viv's eyebrows shot up. "Really? How did you get into that?"

"Through a series of accidents, mostly," Alex said.

Viv laughed. "Just like you got into snowboarding, then."

"Do you still snowboard?" Alex asked.

"Oh, yeah, whenever I get the chance. Of course, not much of that here. I had to come back last year and get a real job." She grimaced.

"You're from this area, right?" Alex asked.

I had the definite feeling of being a third wheel as my gaze bounced back and forth between them.

"Actually, I'm from a little village near Salisbury, but there's no jobs there, so I'm here, working in the bike shop off Milsom Street. You should come by sometime. We run bike tours of the area in the summer." She glanced at the sky, which was clear for the moment, but a few clouds lined the horizon. "Not a good time of the year for it now. I do get back to the slopes whenever I can. Do you?"

"Not really. I have things that keep me here in England now." Alex smiled at me.

"Well, that's…great, I guess. If you want that kind of thing, I mean," Viv said, then quickly added, "And you do. Clearly, you do. You look great—so it suits you." She took a step back. "But we should get together while you're here. I'd love to hear more about this location scouting stuff and catch up. Maybe you could even get me a part in your movie," she said in a joking tone.

"It's a documentary," Alex said.

"Not quite the same thing, is it?" She laughed.

She and Alex exchanged cell phone numbers, and Viv went into the café.

As we walked away, Alex said, "Viv is kind of a whirlwind."

"I can see that. Vivacious. Is that where her name comes from? Is it a nickname?"

"No. Her real name is Vivian, which she can't stand. She'd much rather have Vivacious." Alex glanced toward the thin layer of clouds edging the horizon. "We'd better get at it."

"Yes. No cloudy pictures for Elise."

Alex gave me a rather thorough kiss, which I returned. "See you at the Roman Baths at noon," I said, breathlessly before turning to retrace the path we'd taken from the hotel.

I walked back down the pedestrian walkway, this time taking in the shops and the architecture. When I came to a colonnaded walkway with a frieze of neoclassical figures above it, I knew I was back at the city center.

I turned and walked through the columns into the square. On my right was the entrance to the Roman Baths and the Pump Room, now closed with an iron grill rolled down over the door because it wasn't open yet. Straight ahead on the far side of the square was Bath Abbey. A row of shops completed the square on my left, one of them an explosion of the red, white, and blue of the Union Jack. It was a tourist trap extraordinaire with postcards, trinkets, miniature red phone boxes, and even a life-size cardboard cutout of the queen in a tiara and evening gown.

I snapped a few pictures of the kitsch, just for fun, then turned my attention back to the Abbey. It was still fairly quiet, and I wanted to get my exterior photos while there were less people around. I knew from my research that it was an example of perpendicular Gothic style architecture. Not being an expert in architecture, I probably missed the finer points of the style, but it was imposing with a huge stained-glass rose window between two turrets, or towers. A ladder with climbing angels ran along each turret all the way to the top.

I set to work, photographing the Abbey from a distance, then moving in closer, capturing the angels—Jacob's ladder, perhaps? Then I worked my way around the building, getting shots of each side of it. I made notes in my Moleskine notebook about the orientation of the Abbey so that later we'd know where the sun would be as we planned exterior shots then I turned my attention to the square in front of the Abbey.

I captured it from all sides, then went back to the main pedestrian thoroughfare, Stall Street, and photographed it. I still had almost an hour to kill before the Baths opened, so I found a little café on Stall Street, ordered another coffee and muffin and made notes about what I'd seen so far. I lingered over my coffee until it was a few minutes before nine thirty. I walked back to the square in front of the Abbey, and by the time I arrived, a woman was rolling up the metal grill at the door to the Baths. I scooted over and was the first person through the door.

I paid my entrance fee, grabbed a brochure for the tunnel tour, and went straight to the second story exterior terrace, a walkway that enclosed the square outdoor pool, the Great Bath. I worked my way quickly around the whole thing, getting photos of the pool where steam curled up from water the color of a Granny Smith apple. I wouldn't have wanted to bathe in it, but people had traveled from far and wide to bathe in the odd colored water since Roman times, including Jane Austen's family.

I managed to get photos of the statues of famous Romans that lined the exterior terrace and the entire area before the first tourists, a group of school children surged onto the terrace. I returned inside and wound my way through the exhibits, taking time to gaze at what was left of the pediment of the temple that had been part of the bathing complex. It was only a few chunks of what I assumed were marble.

I had plenty of time before our meeting at noon in the Pump Room, so I moved through the rest of the displays at a more leisurely pace. I lingered over a diorama which showed that in ancient times the Great Bath, which I'd photographed first and was now open-aired, had once been enclosed with a massive vaulted roof. Other more technical displays showed how the water had been piped throughout the bath complex.

I headed off to wander around the various rooms where Romans had soaked, steamed, and cooled off. I didn't take many photos because it was too dark. The cavernous rooms with jumbled stones were dim and slightly creepy with only the distant sound of voices penetrating the gloom. Filming would be a challenge in these areas, and Elise had already mentioned that we would confine ourselves to the more well-known areas of the bath complex like the Great Bath.

By the time I neared the end of the museum portion of the baths, it was nearing eleven-thirty. I had to meet everyone in the Pump Room, which was attached to the bathing complex, so I zipped through the last displays, only pausing to look at a well-preserved head of Minerva, gilded in bronze, that had hung over the sacrificial altar.

After a moment I hurried on, reemerging on the ground floor and took more pictures of the Great Bath from that level, then looped around to the opposite end of the rectangular pool and photographed a portion of the original roof, an arch of narrow bricks. The clouds had indeed rolled in, giving these photos a suffused light, but I had enough of the Great Bath in bright sunlight that I would be okay.

The sound of flowing water drew my attention, and I moved to the far corner where a narrow channel of water swished along. I dipped a finger in it, and it was not just warm, but hot. I crossed the little walkway over it and climbed a viewing platform where I could peer down into the original Sacred Spring through arched windows. The spring was a smaller version of the Great Bath with the same greenish water with steam rising from bubbles.

I turned, and paused a moment so my eyes could readjust to the darkness, then went down the steps of the viewing platform to another dimly lit area with more of the original baths. Those Romans had sure like their baths, I thought as I snapped a few photos. Of course, if you were from Italy, England must have seemed awfully cold, and they probably looked forward to their warm soaks and steamy sauna rooms.

The sides and back area of the next portion of the Baths had thick pillars that enclosed a circular cold plunge pool. It had a set of graduated ledges that ran all the way around the pool so people could step down, easing their way in, I guessed. The water looked dark, but I could see lots of coins winking in the depths as I took a few pictures. This pool seemed especially dark and chilly. I couldn't imagine wanting to take a dip in it. I snapped a few photographs, more for myself than for Elise. I checked them on the screen as I always did before moving on, but I paused as something caught my eye in one of the photos.

The flash had illuminated what I couldn't see in the gloomy light. I frowned over my camera.

It looked like a sock—not a sock that was flattened on the ground, but a sock stretched over a foot.

CHAPTER 3

THE SOCK WAS HALF HIDDEN behind one of the pillars that encircled the pool. Chunks of rock were scattered around the dimly lit area between the columns and the pool. Beyond the columns, the viewing platform with its two arched openings overlooking the Sacred Spring let in some light, but it backlit the space, making the area directly below it almost completely dark.

I peered into the dim recess around the pool, but the layer of clouds had sapped what little natural light there was. With the arched windows above the platform creating a sharp contrast to the shadows below, the area where the photo showed a sock looked as dark as night.

Maybe I'd been mistaken. I went back to my camera and looked at the image again.

I hit the zoom button, enlarging the photo on the little screen. The image became slightly blurry as I enlarged it, but it did look like a sock. It had an argyle design of gray and black—and it was definitely not an empty sock.

I made sure the flash was on and aimed the camera at the pillar again, clicking the shutter a few times.

The light of the flash illuminated the pillar, and I caught a glimpse of the argyle pattern and something flesh-colored above it, but the pillar blocked the rest of...whatever it was...from my view.

I swallowed and looked around. I was alone by the pool. I could hear voices of other tourists, but no one was in the immediate area. I returned to the platform next to the Sacred Spring, but this time instead of looking toward the windows, I went to the opposite side, and peered down into the area around the circular pool.

From this angle I could see more of what was behind the pillar, and it made my stomach flutter like it had when I looked out my hotel room window.

It was a man. I could tell by the sport coat and tailored pants. I gripped the railing for a few seconds. The sight seemed unbelievable, but it was a person, his back to me, unmoving. I glanced around again, but there weren't any guides or anyone associated with the Baths. It wasn't like some art museums I'd visited with docents watching the paintings in each room.

I could hear the voices of a group of tourists getting louder as they drew closer. I gripped the handrail and threw a leg over, thinking that they could get help while I waited with the man. I dropped down onto the narrow area beside the pool and picked my way carefully over to the man, my eyes adjusting to the gloomy atmosphere. "Hello? Are you okay?"

There was no answer, no movement as my voice echoed faintly around the enclosed space. I inched closer, and that was when I saw the long tawny-colored hair that fell to the collar of his sport coat, but my gaze jerked away the moment I saw the bloody dent at the back of his skull. I sucked in a breath as a sick feeling came over me. The man was lying partially on his side, and I forced myself to look back and study what I could see of his face. It was definitely Cyrus. His haughty look was gone, and a startled expression seemed to be imprinted on his face.

I forced myself to step closer and touch his shoulder. "Mr. Blakely?" I whispered. "Cyrus?"

I touched his shoulder. He didn't respond. I applied a bit of pressure, but his shoulder was stiff and the body didn't move.

The body. The thought reverberated around my mind like my voice had echoed against the stones a few seconds earlier. It was a body. Cyrus was dead.

"Oy!" A voice shouted above me, and I started. "You're not supposed to be down there."

I stood and gestured at Cyrus, words failing me for a second as I looked up at the man on the platform. He stepped forward and caught sight of Cyrus. "Is he hurt?" he asked, his tone more subdued.

I cleared my throat. "He's dead."

THE MAN obviously didn't believe me because he pulled in his chin and shook his head. "Surely, the bloke just tripped."

"No. I'm afraid there's no doubt about it." I closed my

eyes briefly, an effort to block out the image of the damage to Cyrus's skull.

Another group of tourists tromped onto the platform, and instead of heading for the windows to view the Sacred Spring, they came to the railing and peered over.

"Do you work here?" I asked the man. "Can you get help?"

"I'm just tourin' the place, but I can tell you that no one is supposed to be down there."

"Well, can you go find someone who does work here? They should be notified as well as the police."

The man backed away, palms up. "I'm not getting involved in anything. We're doing the tower tour at the Abbey in a few minutes."

A woman who had joined the line at the railing looked from me to Cyrus's form. "Is there a problem? I'm a doctor. Perhaps I should take a look." She vaulted over the railing and landed with much more finesse than I had. I traded places with her on the narrow walkway area at the edge of the pool.

The woman squatted beside Cyrus. She looked him over, pausing a few moments as she studied the head wound, then she checked for a pulse. Without moving him, she ran a hand down the side of his body that was tilted slightly away from the ground, lightly tracing her fingers from his shoulder down to his hand, then she did the same from his hip down to his socked foot. I noticed that his other foot had a shoe on it. I glanced around, looking for a lone shoe, but I didn't see it anywhere.

She put a gentle pressure on his shoulder then applied

more pressure until his body moved an inch or so. The upper body moved as a unit, like a toppled mannequin.

She released her pressure on his shoulder, letting the body settle back into the position it had been in when I'd found it. She stood, pulled a phone from her pocket, and tapped a few numbers. "There's nothing I can do."

She looked up at the line of people hanging over the railing. She pointed to a man near the end of the line. "You there. Go back to the entrance desk where you bought your ticket and let them know a man has died in the cold plunge room." He nodded and left as the rest of the group around him broke into excited chatter.

She turned back to me. "I'm sorry. Did you know him?"

"Yes. I met him for the first time today."

"So you spoke to him this morning?"

"Yes," I said, but she held up a finger and spoke into the phone, giving the details of the situation efficiently.

"Yes. Right. I'll wait." She put her phone away and turned back to me. "What time, exactly, did you last see him?"

I had been looking at Cyrus, but glanced at her because of her tone. Her face had an intense curiosity.

"Umm, it would have been about seven, I think."

Her gaze flicked to Cyrus's body, and I couldn't see her expression, but her tone sounded thoughtful. "Hmm. And the Baths are quite cool today," she murmured to herself.

"Why do you ask?"

She hesitated.

"Obviously, it matters," I said. "I can see by your face that it's important."

"It may matter, or it may not. Rigor is incredibly variable."

"Rigor. You mean rigor mortis?"

"Yes. It's already set in, at least in his arms and chest and somewhat in the legs, which indicates that he may have been dead for several hours."

"Kate," a female voice called out sharply from above me on the viewing platform. "What are you doing down there?"

I briefly closed my eyes. I knew that imperious tone. I turned around and spotted Elise leaning over the railing.

"Surely you know this area is too dark to interest us," she said. "Why are you wasting time here?"

"What are you doing here, Elise?" I asked. "I thought we were meeting in the Pump Room." I glanced at my watch. Even with all that had happened, I wasn't late.

"Paul and I finished our meetings early so we nipped in here for a quick tour, but we should move along to the Pump Room." She made a shooing motion with her hand, indicating I should come up to the platform.

"I'm afraid there's been, well—I'm not sure what's happened, but Cyrus is dead."

"Cyrus? Are you sure?" she asked in a mildly surprised tone.

"Yes, it's Cyrus Blakely. No doubt about it," I said.

"What happened? An accident? Or was it his heart? That was it, wasn't it? He was just the sort—you know, too intense. Type A and all that."

"No, it was nothing like that. Either it was an accident or..." I trailed off.

"What are you talking about?" Elise said, her tone

incredulous. Accidents were not part of her plan, thus there could not be an accident. She wouldn't allow it.

I looked toward his body, which was mostly hidden behind the pillar from this angle. "I'm sorry, I don't know —" I broke off because Elise had leaned over the railing to get a better look. She froze for half a second, then surged over the railing, her cape flapping about her like the wings of a huge bird as she descended. I tried to catch her arm. "Elise, don't—"

She shook off my hand and shoved by me. The little ledge was getting pretty crowded. I had no desire to take a plunge into the cold pool, so I stepped back, giving her room to pass. She powered around the doctor as well, and fell on Cyrus's body.

CHAPTER 4

THE DOCTOR BENT OVER ELISE and convinced her to move back, and then several employees arrived. Elise, the doctor, and I were helped back over the railing. The rest of the tourists were escorted from the area, and I saw Paul's form, easily identifiable because of the pencil behind his ear, towering above the group as they left.

The police arrived shortly after that. I learned the doctor's name was Carol Attenbury. She was a general practitioner from London on holiday.

I told the responding officer how I had found Cyrus's body, even showing him the image on my camera. He wanted to take the camera into evidence, but I protested, and Elise backed me up. "Let me email the photos to you," I said. "Surely that will be enough, at this point. I must have the camera. It's my livelihood."

The young police officer frowned. "I suppose that may work, but the DCI will have to approve it. So you're saying you spotted the body, even though no one else had?" His tone was doubtful. "The Baths had been open for two hours."

"Yes, but if you look at the circular pool from the raised platform near the Sacred Spring, that area is extremely dark, and the pillar partially blocked him from view."

Dr. Attenbury, who was standing beside me nodded. "I didn't see him either until she pointed it out.

"And once you go down the platform and go around to the other side," I said, "the area is in darkness as well. His dark clothes blended in. And since his face and lighter hair were hidden by the pillar and the rocks it was difficult to see. I only saw the sock because of the light of the flash. If I hadn't taken that picture, I wouldn't have seen him either."

The officer looked at Dr. Attenbury. "And you arrived next?"

"Yes. I confirmed he was dead and sent for help."

Her straightforward statement cheered the officer, and he jotted it down before turning to Elise. "And you were third, ma'am?"

"Yes. We worked together, Cyrus Blakely and I," she said, her tone indicating she didn't like the situation.

"And you also entered the area below the platform?"

"Yes. I couldn't believe it."

Elise had been standing quietly on my other side, her arms crossed and her gaze focused on the officials moving around the circular pool as they cordoned off the area and set up lights. They hadn't moved the body. In fact, only a few people had gone near it so far. I was sure that would change, but I hoped we would be gone by then. Elise was quiet, her face pale and strained. "I still can't believe it, actually," she added. "I had to see for myself, that's why I went down."

Something about her tone caught my attention. After the discord between her and Cyrus this morning, I hadn't expected her to show grief or even sorrow, but the way she spoke struck me as odd. There was an eagerness to her words as if she couldn't wait to explain herself. And now that I was focused on her, instead of watching the police, I realized she had an almost edgy or nervous aura. She constantly moved her hands, flexing her fingers or wrapping the fringe that edged her cape around her fingers then unwinding it. "You don't need us here any longer, do you, Officer?" she asked. "I'd rather not be here…when…well, I'd rather not be here any longer."

"You'll have to stay until the DCI speaks to you. I'll see if he's ready to talk to you now."

"This is absurd," Elise said, making an abrupt movement toward the exit. "There's no need for us to stay here. They have all our information."

I caught her arm and drew her back. "Elise, it's a police investigation. Don't you think that takes priority over everything—even the scouting trip?" Elise was one of the most focused people I knew, and I wasn't surprised that she considered everything else insignificant compared to her interests, even a police investigation.

"Maintaining our schedule is the *least* of my worries, believe me."

I let my hand drop away, stung at the sharpness of her tone. "What's wrong?"

She opened her mouth to answer, but her gaze shifted over my shoulder, and she snapped her mouth closed.

A compact man in his thirties with short cropped brown hair joined us. "Hello, I'm Detective Chief Inspector Byron. I understand you found the body, Ms. Sharp?" He adjusted his pair of frameless rectangular glasses as he asked the question.

"Yes, I did." I described how the photograph had shown something wasn't right in the area around the pillars. "So I went to make sure. I didn't want to call for help and have it turn out to be nothing."

"Quite."

"I'd be happy to send you copies of the photos, but I'd like to keep my camera. It's what I do for a living."

"You're part of a location scouting trip. We'll come back to that. Emails of the photos will be fine at this point." He didn't consult a notebook or his phone for notes as he switched his attention to the doctor. "You confirmed the death, I understand, Dr. Attenbury?"

"Yes," she said. "Clearly deceased, but I checked for a pulse then sent for help."

"Very good. And your opinion as to cause of death?"

Dr. Attenbury blinked. "That's not my territory. The police surgeon or medical examiner can make a better estimate than I can."

"Nevertheless, I'd like to hear your opinion. I'm always interested in all the data I can gather."

"In that case," Dr. Attenbury said slowly, "it appears he died from a blow to the back of his head, but I only had a cursory look."

"Thank you. We'll be in touch if we need anything further."

Dr. Attenbury seemed to be on the verge of saying

something else, but appeared to check herself. After a second she said, "I'll be here in Bath for two more days then I return to London."

Dr. Attenbury left, and Byron turned back to Elise and me, his hands clasped together in front of him. "Now. Tell me about your visit to Bath, Ms. DuPont. I gather you are in charge of the expedition, and the victim was part of it."

Elise frowned at him. "Shouldn't you be writing this down?"

I repressed a sigh. Trust Elise to get off on the wrong foot with a police detective.

The corners of Byron's mouth turned up slightly. "I have an excellent memory."

He said it pleasantly enough, but there was a firmness in his tone that even Elise recognized. Her chin went down an inch, and her bossy manner faded.

"About this trip," Byron said. "Who accompanied you to Bath?"

"Kate," Elise said with a glance my way. "Cyrus Blakely, of course, along with Paul Alexander, our First A.D.—that stands for assistant director. Felix Carrick, our cinematographer. And Alex Norcutt, another location scout."

"What time did you arrive?"

"A little after six-thirty."

Byron raised his eyebrows. "In the morning?"

"Yes. Location scouting trips require light and our budget is not excessive. We have to do as much as we can in as short an amount of time as possible. We were on the road this morning by three."

"I see," Byron said, faintly. "And your movements, once you arrived?"

"We stopped at the hotel, Bath Spa Hotel. I gave the other...police person...the details. Cyrus insisted we stay there. Dominic and Annie Bell, the owners, are—I mean were—old friends of his."

"You didn't like them?"

Elise had been rolling on in her monologue, but she stopped abruptly. "I never said that."

"I can tell from the timbre of your voice. Either you don't like the hotel, or you don't like the owners."

Elise hesitated for a second then said quickly, "I have nothing against either the hotel or the Bells. I did not like the fact that Cyrus took over the travel arrangements. He wanted approval and control of everything."

"But he was the director," Byron said, a slight look of puzzlement crossing his face for the first time.

"And I am the producer," Elise said sharply. She paused and drew in a breath. More calmly, she added, "I might as well tell you now. It's no secret that Cyrus and I didn't get along. I knew him years ago. I did not want him brought on as the director. We had a few differences of opinion."

Before I could help it, I breathed out a little breath through my nose, a miniature snort. Byron looked my way for a second, and I could almost feel him mentally filing away the nonverbal communication for later. He turned back to Elise. "How significant were these differences of opinion?"

"They were power plays on his part," she said in a dismissive tone. "Like the insistence we use the Bath Spa Hotel, which required a complete change of plans. They were efforts to throw his weight around."

"He got his way, in that case, it seems. Did he also get his way in other cases?"

Elise's lips compressed into a thin line. "A few times."

"And when did you see him last?"

"This morning at the hotel. It would have been around seven or seven-thirty or so. It took much longer that it should have to get everyone sorted into rooms and the day's assignments made. Cyrus was in a room full of people when I left," she said, her voice triumphant. "So I know you won't need to speak to me again."

"Oh, this is just a preliminary interview. I'm sure we'll chat again. And where did you go when you left the hotel?"

"Paul, the A.D., accompanied me to a meeting with the mayor and several city officials. When it ended, I sent Paul to make phone calls. I had some email to take care of, so I stopped off for a coffee at a little bakery for a while to work on it. Once I finished, I came here. Paul and I met up at the entrance to the Baths. Our group was to meet at noon at the Pump Room, but we arrived early so we decided we'd take a quick tour of the Baths themselves."

"What time did you arrive here?"

"I don't know. Eleven, maybe? Ask Paul. He'll know."

"But it was definitely before eleven thirty?"

"Yes, of course. Otherwise, we wouldn't have toured the Baths."

"And what portion of the Baths were you in?"

"The Great Bath."

"Mr. Alexander was with you?"

"No," she replied reluctantly. "He answered a phone call then went off to see the museum portion while I went to look at the Great Bath."

"Thank you, Ms. DuPont. We'll be in touch." Byron removed a business card from his pocket. "Please contact me if you remember anything else."

Elise took a few steps away. Byron turned my way and was on the verge of asking me a question when Elise realized I wasn't with her. She stopped and jerked her head toward the exit. "Kate, let's go. We can leave."

"I don't think so," I said.

"You're free to go, Ms. DuPont," Byron said. "I have a few more questions for Ms. Sharp. She'll be along shortly."

Elise's face was a picture of unease. She didn't want to leave me with Byron, but she'd clearly been dismissed. She finally settled for sending me a squinty warning look before she left.

I refocused on Byron, deciding that while his manner was unassuming and quiet, not much got by him. He asked, "I gather you agree that Ms. DuPont and the victim didn't get on?"

"No, they didn't." I didn't see the use in trying to protect Elise. She'd obviously been trying to convey caution and discretion with the warning look she'd sent me, but I didn't see how Byron could *not* discover the tension between Cyrus and Elise. It had been obvious to everyone on the scouting trip as well as everyone at the hotel. It wasn't something that could be covered up.

"What did they argue about?"

"Let's see. On the drive here they argued about the best route to take as well as details about the production. That was when they both got very upset."

"What were the specifics?"

"Whether *Pride and Prejudice* should be included in the set of episodes we're working on now."

"I'm afraid I don't understand."

"This is the second set of three episodes of a documentary about Jane Austen, her books, and her life. We covered *Pride and Prejudice* as well as *Sense and Sensibility* pretty extensively in the first three episodes. Mr. Blakely wanted to include some more details about them in the next episodes, for ratings. Everyone is crazy about those books, especially about Mr. Darcy. Elise wanted to move on to new territory, the books and parts of Jane Austen's life that we hadn't explored yet. I know it sounds rather absurd, arguing about books written over a hundred years ago, but they were both adamant."

"Nothing surprises me, Ms. Sharp. Any other conflicts?"

"Well, yes. Elise wanted Mr. Blakely to go to the meeting today, but he said he needed to…um… 'Absorb the atmosphere of the city.' He said it was part of his process."

"And why was he the director? Why would he be put on the project if there were issues between him and Ms. DuPont?"

"I don't know. I assume publicity had something to do with it. He's quite well-known. It would be another way to promote the documentary. Look, I have to add that Elise doesn't come off well, but Mr. Blakely was difficult."

"In what way?"

I looked toward the dim ceiling. "It was like he wanted to irritate people. I'm not sure how much of the things he brought up he truly cared about or if he was just doing it to annoy her. He did it to everyone, actually, me included."

"And what did he do to irritate you?"

I saw, too late, that I'd walked into that one. But I had nothing to hide. "He suggested my mother had relapsed back into a pain medicine addiction and that's why I traveled back to California a few months ago. It wasn't true. He had bad information, and I told him so."

Behind his glasses, Byron's eyes, studied me intently. "That's interesting. Thank you for telling me and not holding that back."

I shrugged. "I've told you about Mr. Blakely's conflict with Elise. It would be a bit hypocritical to keep back my own little dispute with him."

Byron inclined his head a bit as if acknowledging the point. "When did you last see the victim?"

"At the hotel. He said he was going to have breakfast."

"What time was that?"

"Probably, around seven thirty, maybe a little later. I'm not sure, exactly."

"And where did you go after that?"

"Alex and I left together. We went to get a coffee, but ran into an old friend of his, so we talked to her for a little while before we went our separate ways. He went to photograph the Royal Crescent and the Circus. I came back here and photographed the Abbey, the square, the pedestrian walkway, and the Baths."

"How long did you spend in each place?"

"Oh, I don't know. It was probably eight by the time I got back here. I spent quite a bit of time photographing the Abbey. It's so dramatic, it will be featured in the documentary. I know it was a little after nine-thirty when the Baths opened, and I was the first person in. I had another coffee at a café on Stall Street while I waited."

"You must like coffee."

"Can't live without it."

"So you've been here the entire time? Since nine-thirty?" he asked, a shade of disbelief in his voice.

"It's a fascinating place. I have to take photographs as well as notes on each location." I lifted a shoulder. "And the museum portion is interesting. I got caught up in some of the exhibits," I said. "I could have moved more quickly through that portion as we probably won't use that area, but I wanted to read the details about the displays. I was actually on my way out when I saw the sock."

"Yes, the sock. It appears we've come full circle. I think that will be all for now." He handed me a business card. "Let me know if you think of anything else that you forgot. Sometimes people remember things later. We'll be in touch."

CHAPTER 5

BYRON SIGNALED TO A POLICE officer. "Please escort Ms. Sharp to the exit."

The officer motioned for me to follow him around the area that had been cordoned off.

As I left, Byron turned to another officer who had been hovering, who said, "Still haven't found the shoe, sir."

"Curious. You've searched the whole area?" Byron asked.

"Yes, should we expand to the rest of the facility?"

As their voices faded, I followed the officer to a raised wooden walkway on the other side of the circular pool. I had been near the end of the tour when I saw Cyrus's body, but there were still several other areas of the Baths to see after the circular pool. The dark rooms were deserted and silent as the officer and I passed quickly through them. We came to an area where audio guides were to be returned, clearly the end of the tour. He pointed to a set of doors. "Exit through there. The door on your left comes out on Stall Street. The Pump Room is straight ahead."

I thanked him, and he waited until I had left the Baths. I wasn't sure where the rest of the scouting party was, I realized. Were we still meeting in the Pump Room? Would they still be there? I checked my phone as I walked. I had several texts from Alex, asking if I was okay as well as a terse one from Elise. *Come directly to the Pump Room ASAP.*

I looked up from my phone and found myself in a bright oval room designed with neoclassical restraint and clean lines. A chandelier glittered overhead. Niches outlined in elaborate trim held Wedgwood displays. It was so different from the ancient baths that I felt as if I had stepped forward in time several hundred years. The low murmur of conversation, the clink of silverware, and muted classical music came from the larger room straight ahead. On one side of the oval room where I'd paused, a woman in black pants, a long-sleeved white shirt, and patterned vest bent over a large book, the hostess for the restaurant, I realized. I approached to ask for the scouting party. Two long curling strands of honey brown hair swung on each side of her face as she straightened.

"Oh—you're from the hotel," I said. "I'm sorry, but I've forgotten your name."

"Mia Warren," she said with a smile. "I work breakfast at the hotel, then come here to work the lunch rush, then it's back to the hotel to finish the rooms. You must be looking for your group. They're on the side by the windows that overlook the Baths. Let me show you."

I followed her into the adjoining room and had a quick impression of elegant columns that soared to the high ceiling, tall windows, and an even grander chandelier, before

Elise blocked my view. She grabbed my arm and pulled me back into the oval room.

Mia paused. "Oh, I guess you've found each other…uh, well. Have a lovely lunch." She retreated to the reservation book. Elise shoved something into my hand. "Hold this."

It was a phone.

Alex emerged from the doorway to the Pump Room and came directly across to me. "Are you okay?"

He wrapped an arm around my shoulders. I leaned into him, a tension inside of me, relaxing. It felt so good to lean against the solidness of his chest. "Yes, I'm all right."

"We're all shocked about Cyrus," Alex said, his chin moving against my hair.

"I'm not," Elise said. "Not surprised at all."

I stepped back from Alex and glanced up at him. "Elise thought he'd had a heart attack or a stroke or something," I explained.

"Oh, that," she said. "That was when I thought he'd died from natural causes. It would make sense that he'd work himself up into some sort of frenzy and bring on an attack of some sort. But now that I know it was murder—that's a completely different situation. I'm not at all surprised someone killed him. He liked to poke and prod, get under people's skin. He was foolish and poked someone who struck back."

"But the DCI didn't say it was murder. It might have been an accident," I said, but my voice lacked conviction. That dent in the back of his skull hadn't been a glancing blow.

"He fell off the viewing platform and just happened to

tumble into that rather hidden location?" Elise said. "I don't think so."

"It is unlikely," I admitted. "But the police haven't completed their investigation. They've barely begun, in fact."

"All the more reason for us to get moving," Elise said. "By the time they officially declare it a murder, I want all our alibis wrapped up in a neat little package that I can present to them."

"Alibis?" Alex asked.

"Yes," Elise said. "Clearly, they've already started the process of checking up on each person in the scouting party. Byron asked you about your movements this morning?" Elise asked me.

"Byron?" Alex asked.

"DCI Byron," I explained. "Yes, he did ask where I had been, but surely that's routine."

Elise gave me a pitying look. "Kate, you of all people should know the drill here. You're a veteran of these sorts of investigations. The police will look at each one of us carefully, probably me more than anyone else," she said with a sigh. "I shouldn't have let Cyrus get to me this morning. If we hadn't argued so publicly...well, I would look a lot less like a suspect. But we can't change what has happened. Must press ahead and get everyone's alibi sorted. Ideally, I'd like to present DCI Byron with a few other leads as well." She pointed to the phone I had been holding. "You take that mobile, and—"

"Elise," I said, speaking over her. "That's a job for the police. They won't be happy if you intervene in their investigation. That's one thing that I *have* learned, as a veteran of police investigations."

Elise had been intermittently tapping on her phone as she spoke to us, but at my words, her head jerked up. She focused all her attention on me. "Kate, you haven't thought this through. I understand you found him, and it was quite shocking, but we have to think long-term. Cyrus is dead. That fact alone puts the production in a precarious place. If anyone else from the scouting party is linked to his death—even if they are only under suspicion—it makes it even more likely that the production will fold. If I become the prime suspect, then we might as well all go home. We're done."

I wanted to argue with her and tell her we should mind our own business, but she was right. The murder of the newly appointed director wasn't good. If someone, especially Elise, were thought to be guilty of the crime…then Elise was right. Most likely we were done. I'd certainly seen projects fold because of less—a lot less.

I glanced at Alex. Our lives and schedules were finally aligned again, working in the same place. If the production went under we'd be back in limbo again, searching for a way to be together. He sent me a crooked smile. "Buck up. It's not as bad as Elise is making it out to be. Some of us have alibis, so that will help."

"Do you?"

"Yes, I ran into Viv again on my way to the Royal Crescent. She offered to go with me and show me a couple of other places we might be interested in."

"Great," I said, then murmured to myself, "Although I'm not sure I'd call that good news."

"What?" Alex asked.

"Nothing. Just thinking aloud. So you have an alibi," I said. "I don't, unless the Baths have closed circuit monitoring."

"That's something to check." Elise bent over her phone, tapping again. "I'll get Paul to look into that. It's most annoying that Paul went off on his own after he took that call. I can't believe that both he and I are now without an alibi. And, of course, Felix is incredibly unhelpful as well. He also arrived here early, but all he can say is that he *thinks* it was around eleven. But Paul and I didn't see Felix when we went through the entrance, so Felix had to have arrived either before eleven or slightly after." In an aside, she said, "I really must assign more work to everyone. I had no idea everyone would finish early. Of course, Bath is a compact city and everyone was doing a brief overview of their locations this morning." She gave an impatient shake of her head and refocused on our conversation. "I have Paul creating a spreadsheet to track our movements. You'll need to check in with him later to give him yours. Right now, I need you to look at the last text," she said, eyeing the phone I still held.

I hit the button to bring the phone to life. A summary message on the first screen had a list of recent activities, which included two missed calls from a phone number that I recognized as a London number as well as a text from the same number. *At the Royal Crescent Hotel. Rm 10. Must speak to you.*

"Who is it from?" I asked Elise.

"I have no idea. That's Cyrus's mobile," Elise said

matter-of-factly. "Go to the hotel and find out who is in room—"

I glanced quickly around the oval room, but it was still empty except for the three of us and Mia. "How do you have Cyrus's phone?"

"It was in the outer left pocket of his sports jacket, where he always keeps it. I've been around him enough these last few weeks during the forced meetings to know that."

"*Elise*, you're not saying that you took this phone out of his pocket at the Baths?" I replayed the scene over in my mind—the speculative look on her face, then her rush to his side, how she'd hunched over him, and how Dr. Attenbury had to pull her away.

Elise could have removed the phone. If she was fast and went directly for that pocket, which had been exposed so that she could reach it. And once she had the phone in her hand, all she had to do was tuck her hand under the edge of her voluminous cape, which was always billowing around, and slip the phone into a pocket.

"Of course I did. We need information so we can control the situation."

I shoved the phone back at her. "I don't want anything to do with this. I can't believe you'd rifle through—"

"Kate," Elise said sharply and glanced at Mia, who quickly looked down at the reservation book. "Careful what you say."

I lowered my voice to a harsh whisper "...a dead man's pockets."

Elise lowered her voice as well and spoke with a set jaw.

"I've already told you. I'm doing this for the good of the production. If we go under, we are *all* out of a job. Do you want that? And what have I done, really? I've only borrowed this. I can't put in a passcode—I don't know it—I simply wanted to see if there was something on it that we could use to point out another place for the police to focus."

"I'm sure they would have made that assessment on their own. Don't you realize you've made things so much worse? They'll look for his phone and when they realize you took it—"

"Oh, they won't find out I took it." She leveled a look at me. "Unless someone tells them. I will give it to the police and tell them I found it in the van. It probably slipped out of his pocket this morning," she said, going for an innocent look.

"What are the time stamps on the incoming calls?" Alex asked, reaching for the phone, his face set.

"Fingerprints," I said warningly. "Don't you touch it, too," I said, but it was too late. Alex had already taken the phone.

"I think we're a little past the point of worrying about fingerprints," Alex said with a sharp look at Elise. "First missed call is at ten fifty, then another at eleven. Then a text came in a few minutes later." Alex used the edge of his scarf to polish the screen of the phone. "It's going to look odd that he didn't check the calls and text message."

"He must have been already...gone...by then," Elise said, looking a little uncomfortable, but then she pushed her shoulders back and returned to her normal, confident tones. "Besides, he never answered his calls or replied to texts himself. He said that's what assistants were for. He would have had Paul answering them this afternoon."

"Then how did you know where he usually carried his phone?" I asked. My thoughts and emotions were careening wildly around, but that small discrepancy caught my attention…maybe so I wouldn't have to focus on other things like Elise coolly taking items from Cyrus's dead body.

"He would look at the notifications when he got a call or message, but he never responded. He'd check his phone then put it back in his pocket. Once, I even told him we could wait if he needed to return a call, but he said he didn't do secretarial work."

Alex had moved on to running his scarf carefully over the back and sides of the phone. He handed it back to Elise, gripped between the layers of material. "Still, it's something the police will think about."

She reached for the phone with her hand inside her cape, but Alex said. "Your fingerprints had better be on it. Otherwise, it will look even stranger.

"Yes, of course." She grabbed the phone, then withdrew her hand back under the cape. "Now, Kate, you get up to the Royal Crescent Hotel. See who is in room ten. Bribe the desk clerk, whatever you need to do."

"Elise…" Words failed me for a moment then I said, "We can't. We can't set up our own little investigation. It's just… crazy. The police will do their job. We should stay out of their way. We have stuff to do…locations to scout, a city to tour."

"The locations won't matter if the whole project is canceled. You of all people should know what can happen when the police get an idea in their heads. Even if they're wrong, it can take them a while to get on the right course. Time matters here. We establish our alibis, and give the police a few new suspects for them to look at. If we do this, we may actually still have jobs come Christmas. All I'm asking you to do is go to the hotel and see who is in room ten. Fine," she said, studying my face, which must have shown how reluctant I was to participate in her scheme. "Consider it in-depth location scouting, which is part of your job. Do I need to remind you of that?"

I closed my eyes. I didn't want to do it, but I knew Elise. She was so determined. If I didn't, then she would. And she'd go about it in a reckless and clumsy way. I glanced at Alex resignedly. He looked about as happy as I did.

"Okay, I'll go to the hotel," I said. "No guarantees, though. I'll see what I can find out, but it may be nothing."

"I'm sure you'll do better than that. Now, Alex, I need you—"

"I'm going with Kate," he said in a voice that didn't allow for argument.

Elise frowned as she looked at his face. "Fine. Call me when you find out who it is. I'm going to check for something in the van, then I suppose I will have to make a quick trip to the police." She patted the pocket where she'd stowed Cyrus's phone before she stepped between us and left through the door to Stall Street.

Alex and I looked at each other for a moment. I shook my head. "I hate to admit it, but she is right about a few things. She's exaggerating some about the police…a little."

"Yes, a bit, but I know what you mean. If the police focus on us, then we could all be out of work very shortly."

"And you know she would go to the hotel herself and that would be..."

"A disaster." Alex said. "Come on, let's get it over with."

We started for the door, but then I grabbed his elbow and veered to Mia.

She looked up, clearly curious. How could she not be when the three of us had been whispering at the side of the room for several minutes?

"Hi, Mia," I said. "You said you serve breakfast at the hotel. Did you happen to notice one of our group, the tall man with sandy colored hair, having breakfast this morning?"

"Oh, yes. He had the full English breakfast, but without the beans."

"I see."

Mia leaned over the reservations book. "He's the one... who...you know...got killed?" she asked with a glance at the connecting passageway to the Baths.

"Yes, I'm afraid so."

"That's terrible," she said with relish. "And he was so lively this morning. Was it an accident?"

"Umm, I'm not sure. The police are investigating."

"How exciting. Did they question you? Did you see anything?" Her eyes sparkled as she asked the questions.

I supposed that her jobs, serving food, making beds, and waiting around to seat people at a restaurant, weren't that exciting, but her avid curiosity put me off. "It wasn't a fun experience," I said and left it at that.

"Of course, you don't want to talk about it," she said, instantly contrite. "It must have been gruesome then. Sorry I asked, but we've never had anything like that happen here. Bath is so boring. You've no idea how I *long* to move to London." She braced one elbow on the book and lowered her voice. "Mr. Bell, he told us that the scouting party had a famous director."

"That was Cyrus, the man who died."

"No! Really? I mean it's ghastly that he's died and all that, but imagine, I actually served him breakfast this morning."

"How long was he at the hotel?" I asked.

She tilted her head. "Until about eight, I'd say. He asked for another cup of tea, which I brought to him, then we got quite busy. He left during the rush. A lot of locals stop in for coffee—a latte or mocha—since Mr. Bell put in the cappuccino machine."

"Okay, thanks," I said. "We're trying to figure out what he did this morning."

"Yes, I'd want to know, too, if my friend just up and died like that."

"Did he happen to say where he was going?" Alex asked.

"The Sydney Gardens," Mia replied instantly. "I asked him if he had any plans—chitchat you know. Mrs. Bell likes us to talk to the guests, friendly-like. He said he planned to stroll in the gardens, then go see the Crescent."

"He didn't mention the Baths?"

"No. If he had, I would have told him to go to the Baths first because they're less busy in the morning."

"Thanks, Mia." I said. "I'm sure we'll see you later."

As Alex held the door for me, he said, "So, reconstructing the timeline of the victim?"

I shot him a sideways glance as we headed to the Royal Crescent, which was located roughly north of the Baths. "If we're going to do this, we might as well gather all the information we can. At least we know what time Cyrus left the hotel."

"With a stated intention of going to Sydney Gardens. Probably no way to verify that. Hard to check up on entry to a park."

"True, but I do know that he couldn't have gotten into the Baths until after nine thirty when they opened. I was the first person in today, so he must have come in after I did." I paused to draw in a deep breath. "I hadn't realized Bath was so hilly," I said as we continued up the street's gradual incline. I had read that Bath was a city of hills, but I hadn't pictured them being quite so steep. We paused at a corner to get our bearings.

"Straight ahead up this street," Alex said. "Then we'll take a left toward the Circus and the Royal Crescent."

"Did Viv bring you this way?" I asked.

"Yes. She said it was a famous road."

I glanced at the sign and smiled despite all the worries swirling in my mind. "Come on. It's Milsom Street," I said, grabbing his hand.

CHAPTER 6

"I SENSE A JANE AUSTEN connection," Alex said as we paced along the road.

"Yes, exactly. You don't remember? You read *Northanger Abbey*."

"I'm afraid my…um…interest in Austen doesn't quite reach the same level as yours."

I smiled. "Nice of you not to say *obsession*. That's the term my mother uses—when she isn't calling it a hobby. My mother is a bit erratic," I added, studying the street as we walked.

"Well, whatever you call it—hobby, passion, interest, whatever—it has worked out pretty well. It helped you land this job."

It was true. My interest in Austen had been a factor in getting hired with the production last spring.

"What's so special about this street?" Alex asked.

"It was the go-to shopping area during Georgian and Regency times, sort of the Fifth Avenue or Rodeo Drive of Bath. Austen shopped here herself, and she used it in several of her books. In *Persuasion,* after Anne arrives in Bath, she first spots Captain Wentworth on Milsom Street." I raised an eyebrow at him.

"Never read it."

"Well, there's another book for your reading list. Some critics say it's Austen's best book."

"Not you."

"How do you know that?"

"You told me. *Northanger Abbey* and *Pride and Prejudice* top your list, I believe you said."

"That's impressive. I can't believe you remember that." I stopped walking and turned to face him. "Do you have a favorite book? We seem to talk about my literary favorites a disproportional amount of time."

"I wasn't much of a reader...until recently. Although, I do enjoy a good thriller. I read one on the last job. Can't remember the name of it now. It was good. Innocent bystander tangled up by accident in an international plot, race against time, future of the free world hangs in the balance. You know the drill."

"Yes, I do. Sounds about as different from Jane Austen as can be."

He glanced out of the corner of his eye at me, smiling. "Different is good."

I smiled back and some of the worry I'd felt about seeing him again after being apart for so many months eased.

A building caught my eye, and I stopped dead. Lettering painted on the building read, *Circulating Library and Reading Room.* "Oh, I must have a picture of that." The building obviously wasn't used as a library or reading room—it was a shop now—but I snapped a few pictures of the building anyway.

"Austen read there, I take it."

I looked through the viewfinder of my camera and snapped off several pictures. "The circulating library was important in her life. Her family took subscriptions wherever they lived, and she read widely."

"I seem to remember lots of bits about books in *Northanger Abbey*."

"You remember right. It's a novel about books and reading." We resumed our ascent of the street. "Reading novels was frowned on in her time. Too frivolous at best and even morally wrong at worst."

"Morally wrong?"

"Hard to believe now, isn't it? But some people thought that the surge in education of the lower classes had been a mistake. Political tracks demanding rights and reform were trendy," I said, remembering my brief detour into post-graduate work. "Novels were popular, too, but they were thought of as a useless waste of time that whipped up emotions and flights of fancy. Catherine gets a little too carried away with imagining Gothic happenings at *Northanger Abbey*." I shook my head. "Enough history and literature. As much as I love sightseeing, I also want to keep my job, so we better get moving."

"So what's our strategy at the Royal Crescent Hotel?" Alex asked.

"You don't think we should barge in there and demand to be told who is staying in room ten?" I asked ruefully.

"No, I suggest we hold off on the Elise approach."

"Right. If we fail, we know she'll do it, so we might as well try something else."

Alex had been studying the shops and restaurants as we walked. "Something like that," he said with a nod toward one particular shop with a signboard out front proclaiming it had supplied floral arrangements to *Downton Abbey* and other film productions.

I caught on right away. "It just might work."

Thirty minutes later, we stood on the sidewalk beside the wrought iron fence that enclosed a row of exclusive terrace homes near the Royal Crescent. Alex held a medium-sized floral arrangement of mums and a clipboard. He had finger-combed his dark hair down over his forehead and had exchanged his brown leather jacket for a plain black windbreaker that we'd found in a shop off Milsom Street. His leather jacket was rolled into a ball and stuffed into my tote bag, which hung heavily, the straps cutting into my shoulder. It also held both our cameras. After a search that took us several streets away from Milsom Street, we'd found the clipboard in an office supply shop.

"Here, hold these for a second."

I took the vase and the clipboard. "Ruffle those pages a little. They should be wrinkled and curled."

I tucked the vase into my elbow and worked the pages over. Alex pulled a plastic name tag out of his pocket and pinned it on the jacket. The name *Bob* was printed on the strip of plastic.

"Where did you get that?"

"I gave the checkout clerk at the office supply place five pounds for it."

"Nice. You'd do any costumer proud," I said, thinking of Melissa. I handed him the vase and clipboard. "You sure you don't mind? I'll do it if you don't want to."

Alex looked me over and grinned. "No, you look much too nice to be a delivery boy. And you don't look at all like a Bob. You're definitely the lady tourist."

"Okay. Good luck," I said, trying to ignore the surge of butterflies in my stomach. "I'll meet you back here as soon as I can." *Is this how the actors felt when the director shouted action?* They always looked so cool and calm. I drew in a deep breath and reminded myself I had the easy part. All I had to do was listen and maybe follow.

The Royal Crescent is a row of terraced houses built in a half circle high on a hill that overlooks a large park, and, beyond it, the city of Bath. The same elegant architecture that was so evident around the other streets in Bath was repeated here. Rusticated stones marked the ground floor, and Ionic columns marched along the ellipse of the façade, rising to the parapet above the third floor. Built of the honey-colored Bath stone that I had already seen so much of in the city, it stood, grand and imposing.

It was a little intimidating—all that refined elegance. To distract myself, I studied the expanse of greenery spread below the crescent and half-smiled when I picked out the ha-ha, the deep ditch that ran along a portion of the park, which kept animals and other undesirables out of the park directly in front of the Crescent. The word ha-ha came up in Austen's works—and I'd had to look it up because I had no idea what it was—but I'd never seen one in real life. I resisted the urge to photograph it, and instead tried to picture Regency ladies decked out in bonnets and parasols strolling along the Crescent, their skirts swishing along the cobblestones, escorted by men in cutaway Regency coats, breeches, and tall boots. Austen had walked in the area, often describing it in her letters.

I reached the central point of the Crescent and spotted a man in a top hat and coat with gold buttons, stepping to the curb to open the door of a Rolls Royce. *This must be the place.* I braced my shoulders and mentally slipped into my confident location scout frame of mind.

My line of work involved cold calls, something that I wasn't fond of, but I'd learned how to do. My first boss had said, "You may be shaking on the inside, but smile and be confident. Half the battle is in the first few seconds after the door opens."

I glanced over my shoulder and saw Alex a few paces behind me. I sailed through the door, giving the doorman a friendly nod, and was halfway across the black and white marble checkerboard floor when my phone rang. I stopped and pulled it from my pocket. Alex's name came up on the caller ID as we'd prearranged. I knew he wouldn't stay on the line, but I pressed the phone to my ear and murmured hello, positioning myself to the side of the room so that I could see the reception desk as well as a hallway and a set of stairs.

Alex strode in briskly just as I had, giving the doorman a quick nod. He was nearly to the reception desk before the doorman caught up with him and informed him deliveries were dropped off at another door.

"Oh, it's just this, mate," Alex said in a passable British accent. "Won't take a moment."

I pretended to carry on my conversation with my nonexistent telephone buddy as Alex turned his brown-eyed gaze on the desk clerk.

She succumbed in seconds. "It's all right. Just this once, I'll take it here," she said extending her hand.

"Brill," Alex said, and I shifted the phone to hide my smile. I wondered if he was laying it on too thick, using the British slang expression for "brilliant."

Apparently not, because the desk clerk signed for the flowers and asked for the name of the guest.

Alex flipped back and forth through a few of the pages, which he had diligently covered in scribbles and columns of text. "She left off the name, wouldn't you know? All I have is a room number, ten. You can work with that, right?" Alex leaned over the counter and said confidentially, "The girl at the shop is new, and I wouldn't want to get her in trouble."

The desk clerk waved a hand. "No worries. I'll take care of it."

"Thanks. You're the best." Alex pushed away from the desk and avoided looking at me on the way out.

I said some nonsense into the phone and noticed the doorman inching my way. I shifted and broke eye contact. I pretended to listen to a voice coming through the phone, but concentrated on the desk clerk as she tapped on the computer then nodded to another hotel employee. She handed him the flower arrangement. "Take this up to Mrs. Blakely in room ten."

CHAPTER 7

MRS. BLAKELY WAS IN ROOM Ten? As in Mrs. *Cyrus* Blakely? Or could it be a coincidence? Was the Mrs. Blakely staying at the Royal Crescent Hotel someone completely unrelated to Cyrus? But then why would he get a text from a complete stranger? I sent a text to Alex and was turning to leave when I spotted the employee with the flower arrangement coming back down the stairs.

"Mrs. Blakely isn't in," he said, returning it to the desk.

"Oh, wait, I have a message here. She wanted a table for lunch." The desk clerk checked her watch. "She's probably still there."

"You think I should take it through?" the other employee asked doubtfully.

"It's always good to get flowers. Yes, take them through to her. She'll be delighted, I'm sure."

The employee picked up the arrangement again and after a few seconds I finished my text to Alex, *Mrs. Blakely*

(!?!) is the guest. She's in the restaurant. I'm going to see if I can get a look at her.

If I could get a glimpse of the woman who received the flowers then I could check online and find out who she was. I was pretty sure I could find a publicity photo of Cyrus and his wife somewhere on the Internet.

I stowed my phone and followed the young man with the flowers to a restaurant area tastefully decorated in blue and taupe. He threaded his way through the tables to the far side of the room. It was quite crowded and another full table blocked my view of the woman seated by the windows.

"How many for lunch, ma'am?" asked a voice at my elbow.

I turned to the man who held a stack of menus. "One. I'd like a table by the window, if you can manage it."

"Of course. This way."

I followed the man across the room to the table next to the woman who was now staring at the flowers. She'd removed the card and was tapping it on the table.

I sat down and sent another text to Alex. *What did you write on the card?*

His message came in right away. *Thinking of you. No signature.*

The hotel bellhop had been hovering at her elbow. "Shall I take it to your room for you?"

"No, leave it." She spoke with a posh accent that carried to my table.

The bellhop left, and a waiter appeared at my table. I glanced over the menu quickly, ordering the first thing I saw, a chicken sandwich. He departed, and I shifted so that I could look at the woman at the next table.

Everything about her, from her Champagne-blond hair to her understated elegant black pantsuit to the leather purse tossed casually on the table, spoke of wealth. She had beautiful bone structure and creamy translucent skin with a few wrinkles around her eyes. She looked to be somewhere in her late thirties or early forties. She pushed her plate away and ordered a coffee.

I went back to my phone and searched for photos of Cyrus and his wife. It didn't take long before I found a picture of them in attendance at a charity event. The woman at the next table was definitely Mrs. Cyrus Blakely.

In the photo, she wore a strapless aquamarine evening gown with a frothy line of ruffles along her décolletage. Her hand rested on Cyrus's tuxedoed arm, but they looked as if they'd rather not be touching at all. Perhaps it was the gap of several inches between their bodies combined with the look on both their faces, forced smiles that seemed to be firmly fixed in place.

I looked for another photo. I knew all too well that photos could capture people in unflattering poses and with expressions that made the nicest people look surly. I found another photo of them together. This image had appeared in a tabloid during the release of Cyrus's last project, a television mini-series set during World War Two. Cyrus and his wife were walking down the street, and the camera had caught them at a moment when his wife had pulled her elbow away from his hand. The look on her face could only be described as angry. Cyrus was smirking. The caption read, "The war continues off-screen for director Cyrus

Blakely and his wife, Octavia, during a recent outing in Mayfair."

The waiter brought my lunch, and I ordered another sandwich packaged in a to-go container for Alex. I figured I might as well eat now that I was here. I dug into my sandwich, noticing that a man had approached the table next to mine while the waiter had been taking the to-go order, which had blocked my view of the new arrival.

I chewed more slowly, studying the back of the man's gray suit and his neatly trimmed thin brown hair. "Octavia Blakely?" he asked as he turned his head slightly, revealing a pair of rimless glasses.

She watched him a moment over the rim of her coffee cup. "Yes?"

"I'm Detective Chief Inspector Byron. Could I have a word with you in private?"

I froze, a bite of sandwich in my mouth, grateful that Byron's back was turned to me.

The restaurant was full, but it wasn't extremely loud. Conversation and the clatter of cutlery was the only background noise, and I could hear the conversation at the next table easily.

"Why don't you join me?" She waved to the chair beside her. "I haven't finished my coffee yet. Would you like something?"

Byron remained standing. I gulped down the bite, and put my sandwich down, ready to pretend to be searching for something on the floor when Octavia left with Byron. I didn't want a second encounter with the DCI so soon after meeting him. I had a feeling that he wouldn't think our paths crossing again was a coincidence. Obviously, Elise had returned the phone to the police, and it hadn't taken long for Byron to find the unanswered calls and the text.

"No, thank you. This conversation is more suited to a private place."

Octavia gave an impatient shake of her head. "I'm sure I know what this is about. Cyrus has gotten into some scrape again, and you've been dispatched to break the news to me gently. I assure you I'm not about to go to pieces. Please, take a seat, and tell me what you have to say."

Byron glanced around the busy restaurant, but didn't turn fully around, so he still hadn't seen me. "Very well." He sat down with his back to me. "I'm sorry to inform you that your husband died earlier today."

After a pause, Octavia set her cup on the saucer with a click. "What happened?"

While I couldn't see Byron's face, I could see Octavia's profile. She suddenly looked guarded.

"He was murdered. Hit on the back of the head. I'm sorry."

She blinked. "Oh."

"You don't seem surprised."

"I'm not, actually." She angled her head to one side as if she was running a mental diagnostic on herself. She shrugged. "I told you, he is—was, I mean—he was always getting into trouble, or more accurately, causing trouble," she said with a grimace. "He had a way of pushing people. He must have pushed the wrong person too far."

"So he had enemies?"

She let out a sharp laugh. "You could say that."

"Can you give me some names?"

"How long do you have?"

Byron's expression must have conveyed disapproval because she straightened her shoulders and became more serious. "I'm sorry to be flippant. Cyrus upset many people. It was almost a hobby of his. I could give you a long list of people he irritated or angered, but I'm afraid it would be sadly out of date. You see, Cyrus and I live—lived—separate lives. We have for many years."

"Yet, you called him several times this morning and sent him a text as well."

She lifted one shoulder. "Common courtesy. I was in town. I knew he would be in Bath as well. We may not live together, but we do talk."

"So you knew he would be in Bath today?"

"Yes. He told me last time we chatted."

"And when was that?"

"About two weeks ago, I think. I called him to tell him I was having the flat in London painted and that it would be overrun with workmen this week. He said that was fine. He would be in Bath."

"If you live separate lives, then why did you keep him informed of your decorating plans?"

"He travels quite a bit, but when he is in London he uses the flat."

"I see. Why didn't you tell him about your plan to visit Bath when you spoke to him two weeks ago?"

"Because my plans at that time were a short holiday in France. My companion canceled at the last moment. I decided I would rather have a shorter trip. I didn't settle on Bath until two days ago."

"When did you arrive?"

"I checked in last night. About seven, I suppose. I'm sure

the front desk can tell you."

"I will verify it. Procedure, you understand," Byron said. "And how did you spend your morning?"

Octavia gave him a long look. "Am I a suspect?" Her tone indicated she was amazed. "Really, DCI Byron, I find that quite flattering in a way, but I assure you that Cyrus and I have rubbed along together for years as we are. I didn't care enough about him to murder him."

"Nevertheless, I need to know what your activities were this morning."

"I shopped."

"The entire morning?"

"I'm very good at it." She named two exclusive stores. "I'm sure they'll remember me. In fact," she grabbed the strap of her leather purse and pulled it across the table to her. She unzipped it, dug around inside, then produced several slips of paper with a flourish. "My receipts from The Cottage and Celeste's." She spaced them out on the table.

"Thank you. This will be helpful." Byron began to stack them, but Octavia put up a hand. "Oh, you can't have the originals. Not right now. I might need to return something. Feel free to photograph them, though," she said in an imperious manner.

After a beat of silence Byron said, "All right, then. This is slightly irregular, but, well..."

"I understand. It's difficult to demand them when you're not sure if I'm a suspect or not. Don't worry. They will all check out."

"But I may need them later—the originals, I mean."

"Fine," Octavia said.

Byron took out his phone and photographed the receipts.

During their conversation, I had gobbled my sandwich when Octavia spoke. Her voice carried and it was easy to hear exactly what she said. When Byron spoke, I chewed more slowly so I could hear his soft tone. I had finished off most of my sandwich and signaled for the bill, intending to cancel the to-go sandwich for Alex. I wanted to try to slip out while Byron still had his back to me, but the waiter brought the sandwich with the bill. As I paid, Byron asked for Octavia's contact information and how long she would be at the hotel.

I picked up the to-go order and slipped out of my chair. As I darted through the tables, Byron commented on the flower arrangement. "Lovely flowers. Who are they from?"

My steps faltered, but I resumed my pace as Octavia said, "I have no idea. The card wasn't signed. I think it's a mix-up. The room numbers were probably mixed up."

"Perhaps your husband sent them?"

"No, I can assure you that is not what happened. Cyrus would be the last person to send me flowers."

I hurried through the lobby and out the door that the uniformed doorman quickly opened for me. I had a bad feeling about the flower arrangement.

Byron didn't seem like the type of person who would write off the flowers. I thought he would add them to his mental list—he hadn't seemed to be writing anything down when he spoke to Octavia—but I bet it was an unanswered question that would bother him. I only hoped it was far enough down his list that he solved the murder before he got around to tracing the flower delivery.

CHAPTER 8

ALEX WAS LOITERING BY A wrought iron fence at the end of the Crescent, his hands shoved deep in his pockets. The thin windbreaker couldn't be much protection from the cold wind that swept across the open green space. Thick gray clouds had rolled in, and a few spatters of rain hit the cobblestones. Alex caught sight of me. "You had five more minutes, and then I was going in."

"Sorry. I had lunch." I lifted the bag. "I brought you a sandwich."

"Well, that's a different story."

I threaded my arm through Alex's. "We've got to move. Byron showed up. I think I managed to avoid catching his attention, but I'd like to get somewhere a little less wide open."

Alex looked back. "Let me guess. Byron has brown hair and glasses?"

"How did you know?"

"A man of that description is stepping into a police car parked in front of the Royal Crescent Hotel."

"That's got to be him. Let's pick up the pace."

Alex pressed my arm against his side where it was looped through his elbow, slowing me down. "Tourists don't jog. Not normally. Unless they are caught in a sudden downpour, and it's only sprinkling on and off at the moment."

"You're right," I admitted. "But I don't like strolling. I feel like we should put as much distance between us and the Royal Crescent Hotel as we can."

"Why? You've done nothing wrong."

"Technically, not anything criminal."

Alex raised an eyebrow.

"I indulged in a bit of eavesdropping. Let's turn in here." We reached a short pedestrian walkway lined with galleries, antique shops, and restaurants. We stepped into the curve of the bow window of one of the shops, using it to shield us from the main street. I dug Alex's warmer leather jacket out of my tote bag. He shrugged into it, putting it on over the windbreaker.

He nodded toward the street. "There goes Byron." A police car cruised down Brock Street away from the Royal Crescent toward the other historic architectural landmark, the Circus, the three elegant terraced buildings that formed a circle.

"Good," I said, and Alex and I resumed our slow pace, giving Byron plenty of time to put a lot of distance between us and him. We reached the end of the pedestrian area where it rejoined Brock Street. "Let's go back through the Circus," I said. "We hurried through there so quickly I barely had time to glance at it earlier." The sprinkles tapered off as we walked, and I told Alex what I'd overheard.

We crossed the street to the round park that the buildings of the Circus enclosed. At the center of the park, a cluster of towering trees were a blaze of golden leaves. We walked around the circle and snagged one of the few park benches so that Alex could eat.

He unwrapped the sandwich. "So Cyrus's wife is in Room Ten. I wasn't sure if your text came through the way you intended. I thought possibly auto-correct had changed a word or something. I didn't expect it to be Cyrus's wife."

"Neither did I. That's why I wanted a look at her…to make sure."

Alex chewed for a moment then asked, "Do you think she was telling the truth, about her and Cyrus's relationship?"

"I think so," I said slowly. "She didn't seem upset at all that he was dead."

"She didn't hate him enough to kill him," Alex said in a thoughtful tone.

"They were still together as a couple, in a way, which is a bit…peculiar. Why not divorce and be done with it?"

"Could be lots of reasons, like staying together for the kids—did they have kids?—or money or religious beliefs."

"No idea on the kids." I shook my head. "I don't understand the sticking together, if they didn't get along. Of course, I've never been good at long-term relationships." I waved my hand between us. "This is the longest I've been with anyone."

Alex shot me a sideways glance. "Really?"

I shifted on the bench. "Yes. Don't look at me like I'm

some sort of weird, undiscovered species. I just didn't see a point in sticking around when a relationship had nowhere to go."

"So you think this relationship is going somewhere?"

"It may have a possibility to, if you stop quizzing me on it." Despite the cool, blustery air, I felt flustered and too warm. "We've been over this. No relationship dissection. I over analyze, which doesn't usually turn out well. So, back to Octavia," I said determinedly. "I think it's odd that she shows up the day before Cyrus is killed."

Alex gave me a long look. "Okay, have it your way. No relationship analysis. Well, not of our relationship—although this is the oddest relationship I've ever been in. Most women *want* to talk about 'us.'"

"I'm not most women."

"Don't I know it—and I mean that in a good way." He crumpled the sandwich wrapper. "So back to Octavia. Why were she and Cyrus still together? Why did she change her plans and arrive the day before he died? Anything else?"

"Was she actually shopping this morning?"

"That's the most important question, right there. Elise will be thrilled that we've dug up another suspect for her."

WE FOUND Elise and the rest of the scouting party in the bar area of the Bath Spa Hotel. They sat around a table at the back corner of the deserted room. Two o'clock in the afternoon wasn't exactly a bustling time for the tiny hotel bar. I had a feeling that most of the time, the bar wasn't that busy, probably only catering to a couple of hotel customers a day, if that.

We joined the table, and Felix shifted his chair to make room for us.

The group seemed small without Cyrus present, but then I realized another person was missing. "Where's Paul?" I asked.

"Making copies," Elise said. "I suppose you weren't able to find anything?"

"The phone calls and text were from Cyrus's wife, Octavia," I said.

Felix sat up straight in his chair. "Octavia? Here?"

"Yes, at the Royal Crescent Hotel. Do you know her?"

"Of course I know her," Felix said, which didn't surprise me. The world of location scouting and film production actually pretty small.

"What was their relationship like?" I asked. "She told Byron that she and Cyrus lived separate lives."

Felix didn't reply.

"DCI Byron was already there, at the hotel?" Elise asked faintly.

"Yes, but I don't think he noticed me. At least, I hope he didn't." I went on to describe the conversation I'd overheard.

"Excellent," Elise said. "That's…well, more than I expected. Well done." The words came out with an uncertain ring to them. Elise wasn't used to giving praise to anyone, much less me. I smiled back at her.

"Of course," she continued in her normal tones, "That information has to be followed up. Here's Paul now. You were able to make copies?"

Paul returned with a stack of papers, which he distributed. "Annie let me borrow their copier."

A rhythmic thumping sounded, then Annie came around the corner from the office in the entry. She pounded her way across the parlor, her crutches swinging. She arrived in the bar and asked, "Do you need anything else? More tea? Something stronger?"

"No, we're fine," Elise said and waved her away, but Annie noticed Alex and I had joined the group and that we didn't have anything to drink. "What can I bring you? Tea?"

"Do you have coffee?" I asked. I wasn't a big tea drinker, despite my time in England. I'd already had a lot of coffee, but I was feeling the three-a.m. start and could use a little caffeine.

"Of course. Decaf?"

"Oh, no. The real stuff, please."

She looked at Alex. "And for you?"

"Coffee, black, will do for me as well."

Annie nodded and retreated, her crutches thudding.

"Hand the pages around, Paul," Elise said, and Paul distributed a spreadsheet. It listed each person from the scouting group down the left side of the page. Times were listed across the top. "I had Paul compile the information we each have about our alibis. As you can see it's sketchy, at best—except for you Alex. Thank goodness you ran into an old friend. We can mark you off the list."

I studied the spreadsheet, which had a lot of white space. Only Alex's name had my name listed from seven thirty to eight, then the name "Viv" filled the rest of the grid from eight thirty to eleven fifteen.

I tried to keep the sour expression off my face. I should

be glad Alex had an alibi—it would be a lot less stressful for him, but I didn't like seeing Viv's name repeated along the row.

I focused my attention on the blank grids and realized that everyone else—Elise, Paul, Felix, and I—didn't have alibis for most of the morning. Elise and Paul had been together for the meeting with the mayor, but after nine forty-five, they had gone their separate ways. Felix had nothing but a blank line of grids after seven thirty, and my line was blank as well after eight.

"You'll have to pencil in Octavia," Elise said, and motioned for Paul to give her the pencil from behind his ear. He handed it over, and Elise scribbled Octavia's name at the bottom of the list. "Kate, you visit those boutiques she mentioned and make sure Octavia was there this morning."

"I'm sure the police will do that," I said.

"But they won't share their results with us, will they? And when will they get to it? Today? Tomorrow?" She circled the pen around the table. "I'm trying to make sure you all have jobs next week. If we can find out Octavia wasn't at one of those stores we can share that information with the police—discreetly, of course—and take the pressure off us. You all know that appearance is everything. I have to talk to the backers later today and give them an update. If we have some solid information about other suspects who aren't part of our group...well, we might get to make the rest of the series."

"But the people at those stores won't give me information about their customers," I said.

"I'm sure you'll figure something out," Elise said. "Look

at what you did at the hotel. Perhaps you do have a knack for this investigation thing. You might be in the wrong line of work, in fact." Elise smiled brightly. It wasn't the first time Elise had hinted I should look for another type of employment. Elise noticed Annie had emerged from the kitchen and sent me a warning glance. I bit back my protests. I'd take them up again with Elise later, one-on-one.

Annie returned with our coffees. Using one crutch, she held the handle of a rolling cart with her other hand and pushed it across the room. Alex jumped up to help her, but she shook her head. "I'm fine. I've actually gotten used to doing this. As much as it annoys me—because I have to slow down, you know—I've found that I can get around quite well, despite the blasted cast." She parked the cart then distributed the coffees and provided a new teapot with fresh hot water. As she placed my cup in front of me, I noticed that her eyes were swollen and pink rimmed.

"Thank you, Annie," Elise said in a dismissive tone then tapped the spreadsheet. "I want each of you to find someone—anyone—a ticket seller, a tourist, a waitress who can confirm your whereabouts this morning. This is critical."

Annie cleared Felix's teacup, which he'd pushed away, then began thumping her way back across the parlor with the rolling tray. Before she'd gone a few steps someone with a heavy tread came down the staircase from the guest rooms, their footfalls drawing our attention.

"Are you finished, Detective Sergeant Gadd?" Annie asked.

"Yes, ma'am. You're sure no one has been in to clean Mr. Blakely's room?"

"No, of course not. He only checked in this morning. We wouldn't clean the room until tomorrow."

DS Gadd was a young man with a round face, ruddy cheeks, and short blond hair, which was standing on end. I wasn't sure if he was making an effort to wear his hair in a fashionably mussed style, or if he'd been caught in a particularly rough gust of wind. "I'm afraid we'll have to search the premises, ma'am."

"Of course, you can look, especially if it will help find the person who..." she paused to draw a steadying breath, "...did that to Cyrus. But what are you looking for?"

He quirked his lips to one side. "I probably shouldn't say, but seeing as how you're being so helpful, and you're the proprietor—you should know in case you find it. It was plain to see at the crime scene, anyway. It's his shoe."

CHAPTER 9

"CYRUS'S SHOES?" ANNIE ASKED. "YOU mean he wasn't wearing shoes when he...when he was...?" She swallowed and pressed her lips together as her throat worked.

"He only had one shoe on, ma'am, when he was found. It's the left that's missing." He consulted a notepad. "A men's black dress shoe with silver buckle and punch detailing on the toe. Size twelve-point-five. Brand, Peter Smythe. You haven't found a stray shoe on the premises, have you?"

Annie had her emotions under control and shook her head. "No. You're sure you checked his room thoroughly? Guests often leave things in the strangest places. Perhaps he changed shoes after breakfast before he went out?"

"No, ma'am, I searched it top to bottom. There's no extra shoe. And that wouldn't explain how he ended up with one shoe in the Roman Baths."

"No, of course not." Annie touched her forehead. "I'm

sorry. I'm still so shocked by the news that I'm afraid I'm not thinking clearly."

"I understand, especially seeing as how he was an old friend of yours and your husband's," Gadd said. "I'll just check around the main rooms, if you don't mind. You said he went to his room and came down to this floor again?"

"Yes." She waved her hand at the parlor and bar. "Please look around."

Gadd said, "Thank you. I'll be as quick as I can." He moved to the far side of the parlor where he got down on his hands and knees and looked under a chair, then he stood and worked his way around the room, checking under and behind all the furniture.

Elise cleared her throat, and we all turned back to her. She kept her voice low as she said, "As I was saying, each of you should find someone to verify your whereabouts. I spoke to DS Gadd when he first arrived. The inquest date hasn't been set yet, but it will probably be in a few days. It's imperative each of you firm up your alibis. If we can all prove we were somewhere else when Cyrus was killed, then the production will at least stand a chance of going on."

Gadd had made a complete circuit of the parlor and paused in the archway that divided it from the bar. "Come in. We're finished." Elise stood and moved across the room to him. "I have a few more questions. If you can't answer them, I'll need your superior to get back to me."

"We're always glad to help in any way we can."

"Excellent. Now, tell me, are there cameras at the Roman Baths? For monitoring, that sort of thing."

"Yes, ma'am, they have cameras, but they weren't in use today."

"Of course that would be our luck," Elise said. "What happened? Did someone forget to flip a switch to turn them on?"

"I don't know. I only know that the director was apologetic about it."

Holding a dishcloth, Annie leaned around the wall that separated the kitchen area. "I can tell you about that, Elise. The system is being upgraded. It was supposed to be done a day or two ago, but they had some glitch and are still working on it."

Dominic trotted down the stairs and must have caught the end of the conversation. He said to Elise, "If you want to know anything about the Baths, Annie is the person to ask. She volunteers there, leads tours, organizes fundraising drives, everything." The phone at the front desk rang, and Dominic excused himself, jogging quickly to the office in the entry.

Elise turned back to Gadd. "Any further word on the inquest?"

"That I don't know. I can have the DCI contact you."

"Do that. In fact, would you contact him now and ask?" Gadd agreed and took out his phone. While he was leaving a message, Elise shifted her attention back to our group. "Paul, you focus on alibis for you and me. Alex, you help Kate," Elise said in a tone that indicated I would need all the help I could get, "with those places we talked about earlier." She glanced at Gadd with a significant look then mouthed the words *the shops*. In a low voice she added,

"Then move on to finding someone who can confirm Kate's movements this morning. Felix, you—"

"Yes, yes," he said. "Find some poor blighter on a park bench who will swear—"

"That's not the idea at all, Felix."

"Might as well be." Felix wrapped his scarf around his neck, which bunched up and stuck up above his collar. He jammed his wool newsboy cap crookedly on his head. "What I want to know is when are we going to do some scouting? You know, work. The actual reason that we're here. Instead of all this larking about?"

Elise gripped Felix's arm and firmly propelled him around Gadd, who was wrapping up his voicemail message. She kept her voice quiet as they moved across the parlor. "You sort out your alibi, then we'll get back to serious scouting. There's no need to scout, if the production is going to fold."

After Gadd ended his call, it only took him a few seconds to search the tiny bar area. He searched around the tables, then went behind the bar area and looked in the cabinets. He checked the trashcan, then thanked Annie for her cooperation and departed.

Elise returned to the bar. I was waiting for her, but before I could speak, she held up a hand. "Kate, I know you don't want to follow up on Octavia's alibi, but that's what I want you to do. You're creative. You'll find a way, I'm sure."

"No, Alex is creative. I'm the logical, practical one and focusing on alibis isn't the best way to go about this. If you want to find out what happened to Cyrus you're going about it the wrong way."

Elise pressed her lips together and blew out a long breath through her nose. "Oh, really? You'd do it differently, I suppose. Well, I'm in charge." She gave me a brief condescending smile. "We're going about it my way. And it's worked so far, hasn't it? You turned up that valuable bit of info about Octavia, which is a stroke of luck—imagine Cyrus's wife, here in town. Even I know that it's usually the spouse who is the most likely perpetrator. No, we're staying the course." She pointed a finger at me. "You go to those shops and get something out of them. I don't care how. And if it turns out that Octavia wasn't there, then go back to the hotel and quiz the doorman and every employee until you find out where she did go." Elise swept out of the room.

I stood still and focused on a corner of the ceiling.

"She seems to have forgotten to issue you a police badge and warrant," Alex said.

"Exactly. That's it exactly. The shop employees won't give me information on their customers. Why should they? What she's asking is impossible." I rubbed my forehead. "But I shouldn't be surprised. This is Elise we're talking about. She always asks for the impossible."

"And she wants it ASAP," Alex said.

I couldn't help but chuckle. "That's true, too."

Alex caught my hand. "Come on, I have an idea. Let's at least make the attempt."

I sighed. "I suppose we have to try. If not…well, it will just be worse."

"Elise will do it," Alex said, voicing my thoughts.

I glanced out the bow windows to the sky, which was still dark gray. "I want my umbrella before I head out again." Alex nodded and followed me up the curving staircase to my room.

"That's a climb," he said when we reached the top floor.

"I should be in excellent shape after a few days, especially if we're not going to be able to leave," I said, some of my frustration with Elise draining away. She was only being her usual demanding self and there was no reason to be grouchy and ruin my time with Alex.

I tossed the paper with the timelines on the bed. "Can you believe that? Only Elise would have an assistant create a spreadsheet of suspects and try to pin down our alibis. I know she's a micromanager, but that's going a little far."

Alex didn't reply, and I looked up from my suitcase as I opened it. He was frowning.

"She is right about the inquest, I think. They can't have it for a few days, and they'll certainly want us all here for it."

"I know. It makes me grumpy when she's right." I found my umbrella and tucked it away in my tote bag. "But she's not right about the most likely suspects. Just because she doesn't want it to be anyone in our group, doesn't mean she can *make* it be someone else." I picked up the paper. "I mean, look at all those blank spaces. Any one of us—except you, of course—could have killed Cyrus."

"Don't leave me out. If this were one of those convoluted Agatha Christie books that you like to read that would mean that I did it since I'm absolutely the only one who *couldn't* have done it—you have odd literary taste by the way, Austen and Christie."

"Austen and Christie aren't completely unrelated. Christie wrote romance subplots in her mysteries, and

Austen put mysteries and puzzles in her romances. And, they were both masters of their genres. But you are right, as far as detective fiction goes, you'd be at the top of my list."

"Perhaps Viv and I are in it together," Alex said, "Maybe she has some strange connection to Cyrus, and we concocted our story of touring Bath—hey, what's wrong?"

"Nothing." I set my tote bag on my shoulder and headed for the door.

Alex stepped into my path. "Something is wrong. You're frowning. Rather fiercely. I know you run from any emotional discussion like someone fleeing a burning building, but I can't let this go, not after it was obviously something I said that made you shut down."

"Alex," I said warningly.

He leaned against the door. "I have all day. After all, *I* have an alibi."

I clenched my teeth together. "All right. It's Viv. I don't like the idea of you traipsing around Bath with her or the fact that she's your alibi. Joking about it just…set me off, I guess."

Alex tilted his head. "You have nothing to worry about."

"Don't I?"

"You don't trust me?"

"Of course I trust you. It's Viv that makes me uncomfortable. Old girlfriends showing up is not good."

"She wasn't my girlfriend."

"But she wanted to be, which is worse."

"Kate." Alex drew me into his arms. "You're who I want to be with," he said. "Viv is a friend from a long time ago.

I'm not attracted to her now…and I wasn't years ago either," he said between kisses.

After a long moment, he lifted his head, and I untwined my arms from around his neck. "Okay, you convinced me. But no more jokes about being 'in it' with Viv."

"I can do that." Alex said.

"All right. Off to attempt another of Elise's impossible assignments."

Annie was waiting for us at the bottom of the steps. "I have a message for you from Elise. She says to meet at the top of Milsom Street at six for dinner."

"Okay, thanks." I hesitated for a second, debating if I should say anything, but then decided I had to ask. Her eyes were still pink. She seemed to be the only person mourning Cyrus's death. "Um, are you okay? You seem pretty upset about Cyrus," I said, feeling awkward. I didn't like delving into emotions and possibly overstepping boundaries.

She tilted her head and smiled sadly. "That's kind of you to ask. I'm sorry I'm such a basket case. I'm just gutted. It's not as if he was an incredibly close friend. We only saw him a couple of times a year."

"But he was an old friend?" Alex asked.

"Yes." She smiled fondly. "I know he was a beast most of the time, but we worked together years ago, in a play. He'd been acting for years. It was right before he transitioned to directing, but since he'd been around so long, he knew absolutely everyone. It was my first play with anything more than one line, and he was kind to me. He helped me get my next job, too."

"What play was it?" I asked.

"*The Importance of Being Earnest*. It was a silly romp, but we had fun," she said with a sigh then waved her hand. "Of course, it wasn't long before I realized that the theater wasn't for me. Dominic and I lived in London then, but then Dominic found this place and wanted to buy it." Her gaze roved to the ceiling. "I guess lodging is more my line. Doesn't sound nearly as romantic as acting, does it?"

I was glad to see her smile.

"Annie, you're boring the guests." Dominic, carrying a stack of papers, came through from the kitchen area. "Let them get on with their day." He pushed through our group and trotted up the stairs.

His words wiped the smile off Annie's face. She frowned and called up the stairs, "Just because you and Cyrus didn't get on doesn't mean everyone disliked him. There's nothing wrong with a little reminiscing about a person after they are gone."

"I didn't realize that Dominic and Cyrus didn't get along," I said, glancing back at Alex who stood behind me on the last step. "Cyrus gave us the impression that he was close friends with both you and Dominic."

Annie lowered her voice. "We used to be. We were quite a foursome for a while there, me and Dominic and Cyrus and Octavia. Those years when we all lived in London, we saw one another quite a bit. When we bought this place and moved here, our friendship lagged, but it was more than the difficulty of not being in the same city."

Her forehead wrinkled. "I'm not quite sure what happened. Cyrus must have said something to Dominic—that's usually what happens with Cyrus. He has—I mean, had—such a rough exterior. He offended a lot of people.

But I suppose he had to, as a director. He once told me that he knew he couldn't make everyone happy so he didn't see the point in trying to make anyone happy. Called it coddling." Her tone changed and became brisk. "But Dominic is right. I'm keeping you here, yammering away, when you have things to do. You have an umbrella? Good. Good. Never go out in Bath without one."

CHAPTER 10

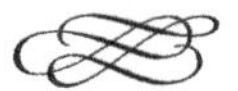

"SO WHAT'S YOUR IDEA?" I asked as we stood outside the exclusive boutique called Celeste's. Alex had asked me what Octavia looked like on the short walk to the shop.

"Just follow my lead," he said. "I'll take point on this one. You can do the next one." Alex held the door open for me.

The scent of honeysuckle enveloped us as we moved through the shop, our feet sinking into the plush carpet. A few racks of clothes were scattered around, but most of the space was taken up with enormous ottomans covered in subtle tones of taupe and cream. A woman with a sweep of dark brown hair falling over one eye met us before we were halfway into the store. "Welcome to Celeste's."

"Hello," Alex said, "I believe my aunt, Octavia Blakely, was in here earlier today. Blond hair, black jacket, and pants."

"I'm not sure—"

Alex pressed on. "I need to buy a birthday gift for her

and this is one of her favorite stores, but I don't want to get her anything that she already has."

The saleswoman's face, which had been guarded at the beginning of Alex's speech cleared as soon as he said the words *birthday present*. "I believe I do remember her. Lovely woman, I helped her myself. She was interested in our dress collection."

By the time we left ten minutes later, we had purchased an outrageously expensive pair of tiny silver earrings, the cheapest thing we could find in the store, and because of Alex's expert questioning we knew Octavia had arrived when they opened at nine thirty and spent an hour in the store.

Alex handed me the gift-wrapped box. "I wonder if Elise will put it down as a business expense?"

"She'll probably return it." I shoved it into my tote bag. "That was impressive. You're so much better with people than I am." He was able to read people at a glance.

He lifted a shoulder. "She wanted to make a sale."

"There was more to it than that. You had her wrapped around your finger from the moment you smiled at her."

Alex gripped the handle of the door at the next shop called The Cottage. "You're up."

"What? No, you should ask the questions again. You did such a good job the first time."

"But then you wouldn't get any practice. You can do it. Besides, it's a guy. You'll do better with him than I would. Just look at him with those big eyes of yours, and he'll tell you anything you want to know."

Alex gave me a little push in the small of my back and propelled me over the threshold into a shop filled with candles, potpourri, and dried flower arrangements. Well, at least we'd be able to get out of here with a much cheaper gift for my "aunt" than in the last shop.

The salesman, a man in his early twenties wearing a scratchy-looking sweater vest over an oxford shirt with dress pants approached, his gaze darting from me to Alex.

I said, "I think my aunt was in here earlier today." I described Octavia and repeated Alex's spiel about not wanting to purchase a duplicate of what she might have already bought. The man hesitated. "I'm not sure I remember her. We've been so busy today."

I looked around the store, which was completely empty of customers except for Alex and me. I shot Alex a glance, the words *dead end* running through my mind. Alex made a subtle movement that I almost missed. Before he turned away to browse the shop, he rubbed his thumb across the tips of his fingers.

"What does your aunt like?" The salesman asked, his gaze following Alex as he drifted to the far side of the shop.

I reached for my wallet. "Oh, lots of things." I pulled out a twenty-pound note. "Perhaps, if you remember, you could show me anything that my aunt looked at and seemed to like but didn't purchase?"

The salesman finally looked away from Alex. The money caught his eye. He looked up at me, a faint speculative look on his face. I smiled widely and squeezed the bill, making the paper crinkle. "Anything you could tell me would be so helpful."

"I see. In that case, I think I do remember her. She was quite torn between the Orange Blossom Explosion candle and the Dusky Blackberry Incognito candle. She went with the Orange Blossom. Perhaps you'd like to purchase the Dusky Blackberry Incognito for her?"

I said I would, then nearly passed out when I checked the price tag on the way to the cash register. I had recovered by the time we reached the counter where he rang up the sale. I hoped my credit card could handle the price of the candle. I discreetly handed the man the twenty-pound note when I returned the signed credit card slip to him. "So she must have dithered a long time over the candles. She was late to lunch," I improvised.

"Yes, she came in right when I came on the floor at a little after ten thirty, and I think she looked at every single thing in the shop." He leaned over the tall counter and lowered his voice. "Between you and me, I thought she was one of those people who look but never buy, but then she bought the second most expensive thing in the store."

He handed over a bag with the candle. Once you got him talking, he didn't want to stop it seemed because he followed me around the counter to the door where Alex was waiting. "And then we had the problem with our card machine," he continued. "It *would not* read her card. It took three tries. I thought I was going to lose the sale. She said she had a lunch reservation and had to leave. It finally went through at eleven thirty, though," he squished up his shoulders, "so, day saved," he concluded, smiling widely at Alex. "Thanks for dropping in. Come again," he called, his gaze fastened on Alex as we returned to the street.

"Well, I think you should have taken that one as well. He only had eyes for you," I said with a smile.

"But you got the job done."

"And spent more on a candle than on those earrings. Over a hundred pounds...for a *candle*. It's just wax, right?"

"Extremely expensive wax, it seems," Alex said.

I shook my head. "Another thing we learned today is that Octavia doesn't have money problems."

"Yes, and it looks like she's got a pretty solid alibi for the whole morning," Alex said.

"Elise won't be pleased."

Alex's phone rang. He listened for a moment then said, "Yes, certainly. Where...? No, if it's that close, I'll walk. Much quicker that way. I'll be there in, say, ten to fifteen minutes." He put his phone away. "My turn for an interview with DCI Byron. I guess they are getting around to the rest of the group. They want to see me at the police station, which isn't far from here." He tapped an address into his phone. "Only a few blocks. Do you want to come with me?"

"No, you go on. I'll visit the Baths and see if someone remembers me."

"Okay. I don't think this will take long. I'll text you if it does."

We separated, and I walked the short distance to the square where the Roman Baths were located. I stopped at the coffee shop where I'd waited for the Baths to open, but the barista and the cashier didn't remember me. I thought the Roman Baths might be closed, but the police must have finished because everything looked normal. A line of tourists were waiting to get in, and I didn't see any notices about portions of the baths being closed. I waited in line, and when I finally reached the counter I approached the ticket seller without much hope. But the woman surprised me when she said, "Yes, ma'am, I remember you. You were the first person in today."

I made a note of her name in my Moleskine notebook and returned to the square. As I emerged from the Baths I saw Paul's lanky figure crossing the square. I waved to him, catching his attention, and he angled toward me.

He slipped his phone into his pocket. "I was about to call you. I've just heard from Elise. She wanted me to tell you that after you find someone to verify your alibi, you and Alex are to go to the Abbey and get some details on the inside. She's especially interested in the bell and clock tower tour."

"I thought we weren't scouting locations until our alibis were firmed up."

Paul shrugged. "It's Elise. You know how she is."

"Yes. Difficult."

Paul's lips twitched. "Apparently, she thinks it might be good for B-roll, and she knew you'd be here." He glanced around. "Where's Alex?"

"At the police station being interviewed." He jerked his gaze back to me so quickly that his ever-present pencil nearly slipped off his ear.

"They took him in?"

He was scared, I realized. "No, they called and asked him to come in. He hasn't been interviewed yet."

"Oh." Paul breathed out unsteadily. "I see."

"Have they talked to you? The police, I mean."

"A bit. A sergeant asked me a few questions at the Baths."

"Then they'll probably call you in, too, today if you haven't spoken to Byron. That's who Alex is with now."

Paul swallowed then turned back to the Abbey. "We'll have to get some footage of those carved angels on the ladders. Very unique," he said determinedly. He took his pencil from his ear and made a note.

"Paul, are you okay?"

"Yes, fine." He shot me a quick glance and an uncertain smile.

"You seem a little…nervous or worried…" I said, wishing Alex was here. He was so much better at picking up on stuff like this than I was.

"Me? What do I have to be worried about? I'm too busy to be worried. Elise always sees to that."

"It's got to be related to Cyrus," I said, thinking aloud. "You've been so quiet and still on this trip, not at all like your usual self. Cyrus did something, didn't he? Did he say something to you?"

Paul rolled the pencil back and forth in his fingers.

"Look, if you're worried about Cyrus making…threats, I guess is the correct term for them…or insinuations about something, then you're not the only one. He said some stuff to me this morning that…well, that made me want to kick him, if I'm honest about it. Of course, I didn't put it that way to Byron."

"Actions are different than words."

"What do you mean?" I thought I detected a trace of bitterness in his tone, but…Paul? Who was always so good-natured, so energetic, and positive no matter how bad the problem.

Paul glanced quickly left and right then leaned toward me. "I know you've been out of the country for a few months, but have you heard of *Criminal Action*?"

I nodded. It was the hot new crime drama that everyone seemed to be talking about.

"I had an opportunity to go to work there. With the Austen documentary up in the air, I was looking around, you know?"

"Of course. We all were."

"It looked good with them." Paul sighed. "It really did. Then Cyrus got involved. He knew some people at the show and told them I was unreliable and hard to work with."

I stared at him. "But that's not true. You're the opposite, in fact. You're always one of the first on the set, and you manage to work closely with Elise—and we both know that's not easy."

A ghost of a smile crossed Paul's face. "Thank you." He looked away. "Unfortunately, they believed Cyrus. Who wouldn't? He's well-known and pulls a lot of weight."

"I'm sorry, Paul. What a jerk. I know you shouldn't speak ill of the dead and all that, but he wasn't a nice person." A job with a show like that would have been a great move for Paul. It would have given him valuable contacts and some security because it looked like the show would be around for a while. Long-term job security was pretty rare in the world of television production.

"You're right," Paul said, his face set in angry lines. "It wasn't enough that he sabotaged me. He bragged about it—brazen as you please. Not one bit sorry. He said I was too valuable to the Austen documentary. He couldn't let me go."

"That is terrible," I said, feeling a fresh wave of anger at Cyrus. "What makes people do things like that?"

"He was a selfish, egotistical sod," Paul said. "So you see, he did more than just say beastly things to me. I'm sure it gives me a motive, at least in the eyes of the police."

"Does Elise know?"

He nodded. "She always knows everything."

"Yes, she is like a witch."

Paul snorted. "I didn't hear that."

I was glad to see the worry in Paul's face ease up a little at my joke. Perhaps Paul's situation helped to explain Elise's rush to find alibis for everyone. I'd thought her motivation was primarily to protect herself and the production, but she had to value Paul as well. As ruthless as she was, I couldn't see her being totally unconcerned about him. She worked more closely with Paul than with anyone else on the production.

He tucked his pencil behind his ear. "Right. Well. I'm off to bribe someone into saying that they saw me at the critical time."

"No luck so far?"

He shook his head. "Zero. I'm on my way back to the coffee house I went to this morning to see if the manager is back. No one there remembered me, but the barista said the manager was on the cash register this morning because someone called in sick. I hope I look familiar to him. Then I can tell the police to clear off when they call me in for my interview. At least I didn't actually get into a verbal argument with him like Elise and Felix," Paul said almost to himself. "That should count for something. I hope it does, anyway."

"Felix argued with him, too?"

"Yeah, I heard them going at it this morning."

"Really? I didn't know that. I mean, we all knew that Elise and Cyrus didn't get along, but Felix actually argued with him?"

"Yes, it was early—extremely early this morning—before we left to drive here. I don't think you and Alex had arrived yet."

"It doesn't surprise me that they were arguing. Felix would argue with a brick wall. He's like that."

"Yes," Paul said slowly, "but this wasn't like Felix's usual bluster. You know how he is, always griping, but he doesn't mean half of what he says. But this was different. Cyrus had just arrived, and I think Felix said something about Cyrus's wife. *Where's your lovely wife,* or something like that."

"That doesn't sound like Felix. He never thinks anything is lovely."

"I know. Maybe that's why it caught my attention. I don't know. Anyway, Cyrus rounded on him and said something about him being jealous. I couldn't hear exactly what Felix said. He was speaking in a low voice. It sounded like his teeth were clenched. It was something about what Cyrus deserved or didn't deserve. I couldn't hear the words, but I could tell Felix was furious. It was one of those situations where you're not sure what is going on, but you know it's not good. I thought I'd have to pull one of them off the other in another minute."

"What happened?"

"Elise came around the front of the van and walked right into the scene without realizing what was going on. She told Cyrus something—I forget what—something about the itinerary, I think, and that set him off. He didn't want to do it in the order she'd planned it. Then they went at it during the rest of the drive, but you heard that part."

"What drama. No wonder the atmosphere in the van was so tense. When you talked to the sergeant earlier did you tell him about this argument between Felix and Cyrus?"

"No. It's only hearsay. I can't even tell you what they were arguing about."

"All the same, you should tell the police."

"They'll think I'm trying to divert their attention away from me."

"Possibly, but it did happen. They should know."

Paul shrugged a shoulder. "Yeah, you're right," he said without much conviction. He looked at the time on his phone. "I've got to get going. It's been fifteen whole minutes since Elise has contacted me. I better get to the coffee shop while I have the chance."

"Good luck."

He loped off, and I went to sit on one of the benches that lined the edge of the square to "have a think" as my friend Louise would say.

CHAPTER 11

ALEX ARRIVED ABOUT A QUARTER of an hour later. "How did it go?" I asked as he sat down beside me on the bench.

"Routine. All routine. Nothing to worry about."

"Really?"

"No, their questions were pointed about Elise and everyone else in the group."

"Did they ask anything specific about Paul?"

"A question or two. Why?"

I recounted my conversation with Paul, and Alex let out a low whistle. "I'm glad I didn't know that before I went to meet Byron. So that's what Paul meant in the van when he said Cyrus had made sure that he'd be around. No wonder Paul was so angry."

"I guess the question is, was Paul angry enough to kill Cyrus?" I asked. "It certainly wouldn't do Paul any good at this point. The damage to his reputation is done."

"But if Cyrus was goading him…emotions can cloud your judgment," Alex said, and I nodded, remembering the way I'd felt when Cyrus had made the comments about my mom.

"I hope Paul finds someone who remembers him. And if Felix could find someone, too…"

"That would solve a lot of problems," Alex said.

"Did you hear the argument between Felix and Cyrus this morning?" I asked.

"No."

"Hmm."

"Hmm, indeed. I know what you're thinking," Alex said.

"Do you? You probably do. You're much better at that game than I am."

"You're thinking that we only have Paul's word that Felix and Cyrus were arguing."

"Got it in one," I said. "Maybe you could take that show on the road."

Alex grinned as he locked gazes with me. "I can only do it with you—and only some of the time."

"That's good. I wouldn't want to be too much of an open book to you."

"No worries there. You're rather fascinating."

I cleared my throat. "Stop. You're embarrassing me."

"You should never be embarrassed by the truth."

I punched him lightly on the arm. "Alex."

"Okay. We'll table the mind-reading-slash-fascination discussion for later—we seem to be doing that a lot, don't we? Tabling things for discussion. The table must be groaning under the weight of subjects we have yet to discuss."

"You're always focused on the horizon. Let's talk about

the here and now. Today. Murder investigation. That takes priority, don't you think?"

"Yes, sadly. All right. How was your alibi-hunting expedition?"

"The ticket seller at the Baths remembered me, but that doesn't exactly give me an alibi. Just the opposite, in fact. It places me right at the location of the murder." I frowned at the church's rose window. "We're going about this all wrong. Elise wants to prove that no one from the scouting group could have murdered Cyrus, but when you look at her rather ridiculous spreadsheet, it's obvious several of us could be the killer. It would make much more sense to try to find out who actually killed Cyrus than to try and prove no one in our group could have done it."

"She's on defense," Alex said. "You think she should be on offense."

I frowned at him. "I don't follow football or baseball or whatever you're referring to, so sporting analogies are like a foreign language to me."

Alex grinned. "Okay, fair enough. You think it would be easier to prove someone's guilt rather than prove the innocence of five separate people."

"Well, not easier, exactly. But logically, it's the thing to concentrate on."

"I'm sure Elise would disagree."

I waved a hand. "Elise *always* disagrees with me. She's so focused on providing the police alibis so we'll all be in the clear that she can't see that one of our group *is* the most likely candidate to have done it. In fact, I wonder if this whole *provide your alibi* thing is a smoke screen." I blew out a breath. "Elise *is* the most likely suspect. She argued with

Cyrus. He was making her life miserable. She wanted him gone from the production. She was at the Baths, alone. She could have done it."

"But look where his death has gotten her. She's worried the production will fold."

"Yes, but if it was a crime of passion she might not have thought things through. Maybe she just struck out."

"And hit him on the back of the head?" Alex asked, his voice doubtful.

"Yes, you're right. Elise seems the sort who would stab you through the heart, not wait until your back was turned and then hit you," I said.

"But that's focusing on means—the way he was killed," I said, looking up at the clouds, which still hovered overhead, dark and heavy, but the rain had held off. The wind was brisk, but the Abbey and the other buildings that lined the square sheltered the open area, blocking the chilly wind. "And we don't know enough about how he was killed to make many assumptions either. What was he hit with?"

"No word on that from the helpful Detective Sergeant Gadd. Elise should have asked him about that earlier today." Alex shifted on the bench. "So, let's look at this your way, logically. Instead of starting with alibis or means, where would we begin?" Alex asked.

"I think the first thing to do would be to find out where Cyrus went this morning after he left the hotel."

"Retrace his steps, you mean."

"Yes, but I'm sure the police are already doing that," I said. "And if he didn't stop to talk to anyone, if he just wandered around the city until he went to visit the bath complex then that won't help us. The next important thing is what time he actually died."

"Ah, yes. If we knew the exact time, then it might winnow the possible suspects even more. Elise would like that bit. Okay, so let's see...he left the hotel around eight and was found at what time?"

"I'd looked at my watch a little before I found him, and it was about eleven thirty. I knew I needed to finish up and get over to the Pump Room. But the Baths didn't open this morning until nine thirty, and I was in the first wave of tourists, so he had to arrive sometime after me. Let's say at least nine forty, which narrows it down even more."

"Okay, so sometime between nine forty and eleven thirty Cyrus was hit on the head," Alex said. "Let's see, if I still have...yes, here it is." Alex took out his copy of the spreadsheet from an interior pocket and studied it. "We have eliminated absolutely no one."

"In fact, all of us were either in the vicinity of the Baths at some point during that time or could have been."

"Not me," Alex said. "I have yet to see the Baths. The closest I came was the Pump Room."

"Which is connected to the Baths. That oval room where you met Elise and me, the door at the far end goes to the bath complex. If someone wanted to slip in that way, I'm sure they could. They'd only have to wait until Mia—the hostess, you remember—was busy escorting someone to a table or making a reservation."

"That's disheartening. I was enjoying being the only person in our group in the clear. Well, what should we do now? Try and help Paul?"

"No, we have a new commission from Elise." I tilted my

head toward the Abbey. "The Abbey's interior. So much for not scouting."

Alex and I stood as a few sprinkles spattered around us. "Now looks like a good time to get indoors," he said as we moved to the pointed arch doorway to the Abbey.

"Alex," a female voice called, and I experienced a sense of déjà vu.

Viv hurried across to us, her auburn braid slapping her flannel-covered shoulders. "I thought it was you two. Imagine running into you again like this."

"Quite a coincidence," I said faintly.

"I had a super short shift today at the bike shop. It's so slow," she said, with a glance at the gloomy sky. "I was on my way home, but then I saw you," she added happily, her gaze focused on Alex.

"It's—ah—great to see you again, Viv, but Kate and I are working." Alex motioned with his camera, which was around his neck, at the Abbey.

"Oh, you're scouting the Abbey?" Her blue eyes widened. "That is so exciting. I'd love to see what you do."

"I'm not sure..." Alex began.

"I know a couple of the guides. I think Thomas is working today. I'll see if I can get him to take us up for a private bell tower tour."

Alex looked at me, and I knew he was weighing the offer. Elise wasn't going to be happy that we'd verified Octavia's alibi and had firmly placed me as well as everyone else in our group at the crime scene. A private behind-the-scenes tour of the Abbey might make her a little less cross when we reported in.

I lifted a shoulder. "That could be interesting."

~

VIV WAS as good as her word and went to track down her tour guide friend after we dropped off a donation and entered the church. I snapped a few discreet photos of the soaring fan vaulted arches and the impressive stained glass window at the far end of the church, which glowed with bright and cheerful colors even on this dim day. The stone plaques that lined the floor and the walls of the building caught my attention next. "They're crypts," I whispered to Alex as I worked out the Old English, reading aloud, "Here lies The Body of Mrs. Hannah—"

"This is Thomas," Viv said in a voice that seemed too loud for a place of worship.

He was a young man with thick black hair falling down to his brows. "I've got permission to let you join the tour I'm about to start. There's only a few other people on it, so it's practically a private tour."

I wanted to take some photos of the stone plaques, but thought it might be disrespectful so I didn't. Viv, Alex, and I fell into line between a family with twin boys, who looked to be about ten years old, and an older couple with gray hair.

"Watch your step here," Thomas said, "the floor is a bit uneven. Graves don't make for the best foundation. Just through here. Make sure to close the door behind you. Thank you. Now, up we go." He touched a length of rope that ran down the central column that the circular stairs curved around. "You can use the cord—it's a rope once used to ring the bells—if you need something to hold on to.

We'll do the two-hundred-and-twelve-step climb in stages, not all at once."

Thomas went first, then Viv, then Alex. Above me, around a couple of the twists of the staircase I could hear Alex and Viv laughing and chatting easily, then the pitch of Alex's voice changed, and I caught a few words, including *Cyrus* and *police*. Viv's sharp exclamation, "Blimey, that's grim," floated down to me. The higher pitched voices of the twin boys sounded below me.

Alex paused and I caught up with him. "Doing okay?" he asked, barely winded.

"And I thought I was in good shape."

He grinned and looked up. "Only a few more stairs to go."

"That's good news."

Thomas escorted us into a small room where we saw the back of the fan vaulting and learned how the vaults were built, then we crossed an open area of the church's roof, dodging raindrops, to the bell tower. "Before climbing the final flight of stairs to the tower roof, we'll pause here," Thomas said as we stopped off in the room where the bells were rung. The ropes hung in great loops from the ceiling. Thomas showed off the modern gadget that allowed them to program the bells so that the church didn't have to depend on human bell ringers to climb the stairs each day.

Then we ducked our heads through a low doorway and took a catwalk through the darkness above another section of the vault ceiling to look at the deceptively simple gears at the back of the clock. I'd fallen in at the back of the group, and I was one of the last to make my way into the tiny space where the light flooded in through the clock face.

"Did you get any good shots?" I asked Alex when he passed me on the catwalk as he returned to the ringing room.

"I don't think so. Too many people."

"I'll wait until the twins clear out and get some pictures."

The boys' fascination with the gears faded quickly when their parents wouldn't let them touch the machinery, and they left. I took several shots of the area, including the catwalk and checked my compass app so I'd know which way the window faced. The voices of the family with the twins faded as I jotted down my notes. I tucked my Moleskine notebook into my tote bag and walked back along the catwalk to the ringing room. I grabbed the handle at the end of the catwalk, but the door didn't budge.

CHAPTER 12

FIGURING THE DOOR WAS STUCK, I tugged and pushed and pulled. Nothing.

I just stood there for a second, stunned. They had forgotten me.

I pounded on the door and yelled, but I didn't hear a returning shout. I glanced behind me along the catwalk to the dimness that cloaked the curves of the vaulted arches, feeling a tad uneasy. I was alone—at least I *thought* I was alone. The corners of the room where the vaults dropped away were in darkness. Someone could be lurking back there.

I gave myself a mental shake. There wasn't anyone back there. I'd only been left behind…somehow. How long was it until the next tour? An hour or so? But that was crazy. Of course Alex would miss me and come back to look for me.

My cell phone. I was more shaken up than I wanted to admit because it was the first time I thought of it. I took it out and was happy to see it had service. I was dialing Alex's number when the door flew open, and banged against the wall.

Alex stood in the doorway, his face puzzled. "What happened? Are you okay?" His gaze scanned the catwalk and the dim recesses over the arches.

"Yes, I'm fine. Glad to see you, though. It's a little... creepy in here alone. I don't know what happened. The door wouldn't budge. Someone must have closed it and not realized I was still looking at the clock."

Alex ducked his head back out the small door and called, "I found her."

I followed him out the door, pausing to close it behind me. The handle worked fine on this side.

"It wasn't the handle." Alex nudged a doorstop with his toe. It was a few inches away from the door. "The door didn't open the first time I tried it, then I saw this wedged up against it."

"That couldn't have been an accident. Who puts a door stop against a door that's already closed?"

I heard a stifled giggle and looked over Alex's shoulder to see the twin boys whispering. The dad leaned over them. "Did you do that? Did you lock that nice lady in the clock tower?"

Both boys shook their heads. The parents exchanged a glance, then the mom took a hesitant step toward me. "I'm so sorry, if they—"

Viv pushed through their group. "Oh my gosh. What happened? Where were you?"

I took pity on the mom—she looked so embarrassed—and said, "It's okay. The door must have gotten stuck...or something." I watched the boys, but they both fixed me with a double whammy of wide-eyed innocent looks.

Viv said, "We looked around, and it was like you'd just vanished. So weird."

"Yes. Very strange."

~

"AND THE REST of the tour was anticlimactic," I said as we finished dinner later that night. The scouting group was gathered around a table in O'Toole's Pub. Except for the dark beams overhead, we could have been dining at a Chili's. The menu had everything from a chicken club sandwich to a variety of salads. Televisions in the corners broadcast sports, but it was soccer instead of football or baseball.

"I imagine everything comes as a letdown after being rescued," Melissa said. She'd finished for the day at the Fashion Museum and had joined our group for dinner. I thought she'd added a new eyebrow ring since the last time I'd seen her, but her short hair was still blond, except for her bangs, which were dyed fuchsia. Today she wore a leather jacket with steampunk overtones along with dress pants in a houndstooth check and ankle boots.

"But did you get anything useful for a possible feature?" Elise asked.

"Yes, there's plenty there we can use. The stained glass and vaulted ceiling are gorgeous," I said. "And we can use the views from the tower for some panoramic scenes of Bath. You can see so much from there—even down into the Roman Baths."

"Good," Elise said. "Email me a report before tomorrow morning."

I glanced at Alex. I knew what we'd be doing the rest of the night.

"Now, about tomorrow," Elise said. "Since no one has had any success in establishing an alibi—and some of us have even taken a step back in that area," she said with a glance at Alex and me, "I want each of you to retrace your steps exactly, tomorrow morning. I hope that revisiting the same places at the same time of day will give you a better result," she frowned at us as if it was our fault that we couldn't find someone to document all our movements that morning. "Felix, you'll be glad to know that in the afternoon, we'll get back to work. The weather is supposed to be good, so we'll visit Box Hill and then check some hotel possibilities."

Box Hill was the picnic site in *Emma,* and while we weren't exactly close to it in Bath, we were closer than we would normally be in Derbyshire and Elise wanted to take a look at it. It was one of the excursions that Cyrus had objected to, saying we shouldn't waste our time traveling about the countryside and should focus on Bath, but now that he was gone it was back on the agenda.

The waitress cleared our plates, and we began to bundle into our coats. "Where are my gloves?" Elise asked of no one in particular as she patted her pockets. "I must have left them in the hotel," she muttered as we moved to the door.

"The last time I saw them was in the hotel," Paul said.

I'd tried to engage Paul in conversation during dinner, but he'd been distracted and withdrawn. He said he hadn't received a call to provide a statement to the police, so I thought he was still worried about that.

"Well, they'll turn up," Elise said. "They have my initials embroidered on them so I doubt someone else took them by mistake. They are probably still on the table in the parlor at the hotel."

On the street outside the pub, Elise left our group, saying she was meeting a friend for a drink. As we strolled back to the hotel, Alex set a pace that separated us from Paul, Felix, and Melissa. The Christmas lights were up, strung across the street from rooftop to rooftop, but not lit. "I wish the lights were on. It would make some great photos," I said.

"Nothing we could use for the documentary."

"No, they'd be pictures just for me."

"Anyone up for a drink?" Felix called as we turned onto the street with the Bath Spa Hotel. We turned back to see the three of them had stopped in front of a bar.

Alex looked at me with raised eyebrows. I shook my head. "I'd rather put that report together for Elise with a clear head. You go ahead if you want. I'll do a rough draft, and you can proof it."

"No, I'll come with you." Alex turned back to the group. "We're ditching you slackers to get some work done."

Melissa linked her arms through Paul's and Felix's elbows. "Then it's just you and me, boys."

ALEX and I set up our computers in the parlor area and compiled the report for Elise. Then we spent the rest of the evening warming our feet at the fire that Dominic built for us and sipping a mug of hot chocolate, which Annie insisted we have. It had been a long day and the emotional strain, not to mention traipsing all over Bath, had worn me out. I was snuggled into my chair with my head tilted back, letting the fire mesmerize me.

Alex had gone upstairs to get a spare memory card for his camera when Annie came into the parlor and went over to the circular iron staircase that curved down to the basement. "Dominic?" she called then turned to me. "Sorry to shout—terribly impolite, but we don't have an intercom."

"It's fine. You're not bothering me."

Annie tapped the railing for a second then muttered something about Dominic going out without telling her. She propped her crutches up on the wall and hopped down from the first step to the second on her good foot as she kept her leg with the cast tucked up at the knee.

I jumped up. "Can I help? That doesn't look safe at all."

"I'm sure it's not," Annie said, "but needs must and all that."

"Well, you don't need to. I'll be happy to help, if I can. Can I bring something up for you or just check that Dominic isn't down there?"

"Oh, he's not down there. He did mention earlier this evening that he needed to run over to the pub next door for some flyers, so I'm sure that's where he is. I need a stack of bills on the corner of the desk. If you could..."

"Of course. Not a problem."

We changed places, and I went down the spiral with Annie leaning over the banister, apologizing for the inconvenience. As I reached the bottom step, she said, "When you come off the stairs, the WC is to the right, and the office is the door straight ahead. Is it locked?"

I tried the handle on the metal door with a rectangle of glass inset. "It's open."

"Good. Just go on in. A stack of mail should be on the corner of the desk under a paperweight. I need everything in that stack. Just bring up the whole thing."

The desk had several untidy piles of paper on it, but only one had a thick square stone on top of them. "I see them," I said, and removed the papers from under the stone. "That's some paperweight," I called out.

"It's a cobblestone," Annie said. "Dominic talked one of the workers into giving it to him when they repaired the road last year. He's quite proud of it. Take a look around while you're in the office. Check out the vault. It's the thick metal door next to the storage room. I'm surprised Dominic hasn't given your group the tour—the two-bit tour I call it."

The desk filled the space near the door, but on the wall opposite it were two more doors. One was made with aged wood and had an arched shape, but the panels looked solid. A shiny modern latch was affixed to the door, the bolt shot home into the doorframe—the storage room, I assumed. Next to it was a metal door about four feet high set into the wall. A circular silver handle was mounted at the center of the door. "That looks like something you'd see in a bank," I said as I came out of the office, closing the door behind me.

"It is. This building was a casino once. All the money and chips were stored down there every night," Annie said as I climbed the steps. "I'd open it for you, but Dominic has the key. The vault walls are several inches thick. Needless to say, it came with the building. This building was once a tannery, too, long before it was a casino. And it was divided into several residences at one point as well."

"That's fascinating, all the different incarnations it's had," I said, seeing that Alex had returned.

As I handed off the papers to Annie, she said to Alex, "Would you like to take a look downstairs? It's not as old as the Roman Baths, but it is interesting."

Alex declined, and Annie insisted on refreshing our hot chocolate before going to pay her bills.

It was after eleven when Melissa sailed into the hotel. She entered along with a gust of cold air and waggled a hand at Alex and me. "See you bright and early in the morning, darlings. I have very important nana—, mannequins," she corrected, enunciating each syllable carefully, "to clothe tomorrow. Must get some sleep."

I put my nearly empty mug of hot chocolate down. "I'll be sure she makes it up the stairs," I said in an undertone to Alex.

I caught Melissa's arm as she wavered on the third step and helped her up the tight spiral to the rooms on the upper floors. "That Cyrus—he was awful," she said. "Paul told me all about it. Did you hear how awful Cyrus was?"

"Some of it, yes. What did Paul tell you?"

"That Cyrus was awful."

"In what way?" I asked, curious if he'd told Melissa the same thing that he'd told me.

She paused on a step and pushed her finger into my shoulder to emphasize her point. "Just awful."

"Yes, you said that. Did he say what happened?"

"I'm so glad I don't work for him. He's awful."

"So I've heard," I said and gave up trying to get information out of Melissa and instead concentrated on getting her up the stairs.

MELISSA WAS MORE coherent in the morning. I came out of the bathroom and found her sitting up in bed rubbing her hand across her face. Fuchsia and blond strands of her short hair stood out around her head. Her black eyeliner was smeared under her eyes and across one cheek.

"Hey. Need an aspirin?"

She groaned and flopped back onto the bed then groaned again.

I found an aspirin, poured her a glass of water and took them to her. "Here. Take these. You have very important mannequins to clothe today."

"Do I?" The pillow muffled her reply.

"That's what you said last night."

"Oh." She turned her head slightly so that I could see one black-smudged eye. "What else did I say?"

"Not much actually. You said Cyrus was awful."

"Nothing about Paul?"

"Only that Cyrus was awful to Paul."

"Thank goodness."

I tilted my head. "What are you worried about?"

"Nothing. Forget it." A blush tinged her cheeks.

I wondered...was Melissa into Paul? She'd never talked about him before, not in that way. But for all her openness, she played certain things close to the vest.

"What did Paul say about Cyrus?"

She struggled up on an elbow. "What about Paul?" She focused on the aspirin. "What are those for?"

"Your hangover."

"I'm not hungover. I'm always like this in the morning," she said but downed them anyway.

"What did Paul tell you about Cyrus?"

"That he made sure Paul didn't get hired at *Criminal Actions*. Can you believe it? The ego of that man. Cyrus, I mean."

"Paul mentioned it yesterday. It's horrible, I know, but the upside is that Paul is still on the crew and here in Bath."

Her cheeks flushed a brighter pink. "Um, yeah. Right. Whatever. Are you done in the shower?"

"All yours. I'm going down to breakfast."

She threw back the covers, put a hand to her forehead, and headed for the bathroom.

I WENT DOWN THE STAIRS, through the kitchen area where Dominic, Annie, and Mia were working, and into the dining room. All of the tables were empty except for one, but several customers, who appeared to be locals, were waiting for their coffees and lattes then leaving as they were handed out. I touched the chair across from Felix, and he waved a hand. "Please, join me. If you can stand my crabbiness before I've had a second cup of coffee."

"I haven't had one cup, so I'm probably more crabby than you."

"I doubt that."

My back was to the door to the kitchen, but Felix raised

his hand, and Mia in her hotel apron over a polo shirt and jeans, popped over to our table, coffeepot in hand. "Good morning. Would you like to see a menu?" she asked.

"Just coffee for now," I said.

"There's a buffet to start." Her chestnut hair was caught back in a ponytail, but her two signature strands of curls shifted on either side of her animated face as she nodded at a wooden dresser in the far corner with a spread of cereals and pastries.

"Thank you. I'll wait a bit."

Mia said, "Fine. Fine. Just let me know when you're ready to order. We do a full English breakfast that's quite good."

She left, and Felix muttered, "Can't stand all that jolliness so early in the morning. Makes me testy. Alex will be down soon."

I nodded and sipped my coffee. After half a cup I felt more like my normal self and ordered pancakes. "I'll have the same," Felix said to Mia.

Mia brought our food, and Felix ate quickly. Alex showed up, ordered eggs, and went to examine the buffet.

Felix angled his silverware across his plate. Before he could push away from the table, I asked, "With all the commotion yesterday, I never got to hear your answer about Octavia."

He'd been dabbing his mouth with his napkin when I spoke. He froze, the linen pressed to his lips. "Octavia?" He put the napkin down slowly.

"Yes, what did you think of the relationship between Octavia and Cyrus? She told Byron they lived separate lives."

He fussed with the napkin, tucking it carefully under the edge of his plate. "I've never understood why she married him," he said quietly without a trace of his usual bluster. "It doesn't surprise me that they were living apart. Who could live with Cyrus?" His chair screeched over the hardwood floor as he stood. "Don't know how anyone could stand the arrogant fool."

"What's his problem?" asked Paul, who had just arrived, after stepping aside to let Felix pass him.

"I asked him about Octavia and Cyrus," I said.

Alex returned to the table with two glasses of orange juice. "Fresh squeezed." He put one in front of me before he took a seat beside me.

"Thanks."

Alex tilted his head toward the doorway where Felix had left. "Still his usual irritable self, I see."

"Yes. He didn't want to talk about Cyrus and Octavia."

Annie arrived, balanced on a single crutch, with Alex's plate of eggs in her free hand. She deposited it in front of Alex, and took Paul's order.

"Poor lamb," Annie said, looking after Felix as he disappeared around the corner on his way to the stairs. "He's always been sensitive about Octavia. At least, that's what I've heard, and it seems to be true. I'd never met Felix until yesterday. I'd heard about him, from Cyrus. Felix and Cyrus used to work together quite often," She looked over her shoulder as if checking to make sure Felix hadn't returned. "I always thought it was a shame—"

The ring of a landline phone sounded in the distance. Annie listened for a second then sighed. "That digital answering service is always going wonky. Excuse me, I'll have to answer it in the office."

I speared a bite of pancake after she left. "Interesting how the theater keeps popping—"

A scream cut through the air.

CHAPTER 13

ALEX, PAUL, AND I WERE paralyzed for a second. There was something primitive and raw about that scream that sent a cold shock of fear through me. The scream tapered off, then in the complete silence that followed, I could faintly hear someone breathing in a labored way, gulping in air.

We all moved at once. Silverware dropped. Chairs scraped. We surged to the doorway and through the empty kitchen area, with Alex in the lead. He pushed by Elise, who was stepping off the staircase. "What was that horrible noise?"

I was a pace behind him, and ignored her, too, my attention focused on the parlor, which was the direction the scream had come from, but it was empty.

Beyond it, in the entry, I could see Annie's crutch on the floor. We moved into the small square of space between the hotel's door and the little office alcove with the reception desk.

Annie sagged against the doorframe of the office, the muscles of her back working with her strained breathing.

Alex said, "Annie, is something wrong? Can we do—"

He stopped dead for a moment, then glanced over his shoulder at me. "Call an ambulance. Quickly." His voice was strained, and his face had gone pale.

I patted my pockets. "My phone. It's in my room."

I turned to get it, but Paul, who was right behind me said, "I've got mine. I'll do it."

Alex stepped around Annie and went into the small room.

I followed and had intended to put my hand on Annie's shoulder and ask what was wrong, but one glance inside the door brought me to a complete standstill.

Graffiti was my first thought as I took in the red spatters on the walls and the floor, then almost the next second a coppery smell hit me, and the thought flashed through my mind that it wasn't paint. It was blood.

I felt a roaring in my ears as I looked at the pools of blood on the floor, thick and shiny. It was too much blood. The sight of it spreading slowly across the wooden planks of the floor was shocking. My mind couldn't seem to process anything clearly. Fragmented thoughts skittered through my brain. *Too much. Horrible.* A crumpled form lay on the floor. I recognized the hotel apron, the jeans, and the long chestnut ponytail. Mia. Her back was to the door, and her arms and legs were sprawled at awkward angles.

The room was barely big enough for Alex to go inside. He stepped carefully across Mia, pushing in the rolling desk chair, which was positioned a few inches away from the desk. As he pushed the chair back into the kneehole of the desk, it closed the middle lap drawer of the desk, which had been pulled out. Alex kneeled beside Mia and put out a hand, then drew it back quickly.

"Is she—" I broke off as Alex looked toward me and gave a small shake of his head.

Annie sucked in another shuddering breath, and I said, "Annie. Here, let me help you. You should sit down."

She gripped the doorframe, clinging to it, leaving a red print on the white trim. She turned her face toward me, but her gaze was vacant.

"Paul, help me," I said as I took Annie by the shoulders and edged her away from the office.

Annie swung around obediently, smearing a streak of blood on my sleeve. Paul grabbed her other side. The cast and her befuddled state made movement awkward, but we got her into the parlor area and into a chair.

Paul got a quick glance at the office before we moved away and muttered something under his breath then looked at me over Annie's head after she was seated. "What happened?"

I shook my head, too upset to speak.

Annie sat completely still, her gaze fixed on her hands. Only one hand, her left one, was red, I realized. "I switched on the light and there she was." Annie breathed heavily for a moment. "We never turn the light off during the day. Who would have turned the light off?" She flexed her hands, which were resting palm up on her knees. The blood on her hand was drying, cracking in the creases of her skin on her fingers and palm.

Elise, who must have looked into the office area once Paul and I maneuvered Annie away, returned to the parlor, her skin an ashy color. "Someone called for an ambulance?" she asked.

"I did. On the way," Paul said. "In fact, I think I hear it. I'll go meet it." Paul left through the front door.

Felix came down the stairs and into the parlor. "What's all the fuss—" He frowned at Annie's bright red hand. "Has there been an accident?"

"Something like that," Elise said.

Melissa, freshly showered and with her hair still damp, breezed down the stairs and made for the hotel door. She saw me and said, "I'm off. See you later..." her words tapered off like a clock winding down as her gaze traveled from me to Annie to the other still people in the room, finally coming to rest on Alex who had just emerged from the office. The knees of his jeans were soaked with blood.

Elise said to Melissa, "You can't leave. I'm sure the police will want to speak to you. To all of us, in fact."

Melissa blinked.

Elise waved a hand at Melissa and Felix, "Best have a seat." She looked at Annie critically. "She needs a brandy," she said and went into the bar.

Elise was right, I realized. The hotel was a crime scene. Someone had killed Mia. I lowered myself into a club chair, my thoughts whirling. Another murder.

The clatter of glassware sounded as Alex came over and sat down beside me. He reached out a hand, and I gripped it tightly, noticing that his hands were clear of any blood. "What happened?"

Alex's face looked even more washed out than it had before. "Someone cut her throat," he said quietly. "I was going to check for a pulse, but I...couldn't."

I closed my eyes. It was incredible...unbelievable.

I squeezed Alex's hand tighter.

Elise returned with a glass and told Annie to drink it. "It's brandy," Elise said, but Annie only stared at the glass.

"Go on, drink up," Elise said. Annie automatically took a sip, then sputtered. "One more," Elise ordered. "Good. Now, I think you need this." Elise pulled off her black cape that had been fluttering around her as she moved. She draped it over Annie's shoulders and nodded. She scanned Alex's face. "You could do with a drink as well," she said and was off to the bar again.

The alternating high-low pitch of the ambulance siren grew much louder then cut off. Paul escorted the emergency crew inside and showed them the office alcove.

They came out almost immediately.

"She couldn't have been more than twenty," I said, thinking of Mia's bright, eager face.

"Nineteen," Annie said suddenly. She held the brandy close to her chest with her clean hand, her gaze focused on the empty fireplace. "She was a good worker. Except for that spot of bother with Mr. Gaston's watch. She settled down after that and gave us no problems." No one said anything to her, but Annie kept talking, addressing the fireplace in a singsong voice. "It was a few weeks after she started. His watch went missing. Mrs. Gaston insisted that she saw Mia poking about their belongings when she came in the room unexpectedly, but Mia turned out her pockets immediately and let them search her bag." Annie lifted a shoulder. "What could they do then?" Annie looked toward me. "There's always a guest or two who try to take advantage."

"I'm sure there are," I said while thinking *she's in shock*.

Elise brought a brandy for Alex. As he thanked her for it, Dominic came in the open front door with a plastic bag in one hand. "What's happened? Is someone hurt? I saw the ambulance—"

Annie shifted toward him, her gaze seeming to come into focus for the first time. "Oh, Dominic," she said in her normal voice. "It's so awful. Someone's cut Mia's throat."

"What?" he moved across the room to her, his gaze quickly running around our faces.

She nodded. "It's true. There's blood," she stopped and swallowed thickly, "all over the office. Someone cut her throat."

Dominic looked back to the entry where the emergency crew now stood in front of the door. "Surely...an accident..."

Annie shook her head. "No," she said. "I saw it all. All the blood. Someone cut her throat with the little Swiss army knife, the one we keep in the desk. I saw it there on the floor, right beside her. It was bloody, too. Absolutely coated."

CHAPTER 14

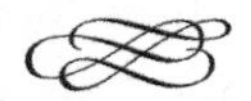

SOON ANOTHER SIREN SOUNDED AND then the police arrived, uniformed men. I knew they were only the first wave. Eventually, after much activity, we were all escorted into the dining room and told to wait without talking to each other or using our phones. Alex was allowed to change into a new pair of jeans, but the police kept his blood-soaked ones, depositing them in an evidence bag. I caught a few glimpses of the investigating officers and spotted Byron.

The minutes dragged by. There was nothing to do but think, and my mind was humming, wondering why someone would kill Mia and if—how?—it was related to Cyrus's death. Because the two deaths must be related, surely? I didn't know much about the crime statistics in Bath, but I doubted that homicide was *that* common.

One by one, our group was called for individual interviews. Annie, who was still huddled in Elise's cape, was first, then Dominic. Alex was called next, and I was after him. I passed Alex on his way out of the bar area of the hotel. "I'll wait for you in the dining room," he said, and I nodded as I followed Gadd.

Byron was waiting in the back of the bar area as far away from the commotion at the entry of the hotel as possible. People were still moving around the entry and the parlor, as well as in and out of the hotel. The front door was propped open, letting in a cold draft. A camera flash illuminated a wall as I walked by.

I settled onto the chair across the table from Byron. I supposed this was the only place left in the hotel for him to speak to people. We'd filled all the rooms upstairs. The ground floor was taken up with our group waiting in the dining room and the police investigators had spilled over from the entry into the parlor area.

"You were the third person to arrive on the scene?" Byron asked. He wore another unremarkable dark suit, but he looked tired. Dark circles shadowed his eyes, and his glasses had a smudge on the corner. The table in front of him was blank. No notebook or phone or computer tablet in sight.

"Yes. I came in with Alex. He went into the office to check on Mia."

"But you did not?"

"No. It was too crowded."

"Tell me what happened."

I summarized the awful sight and how I had first mistaken it for graffiti. When I finished, he nodded.

"And before this, when did you see Ms. Warren last?"

It took me a second to work out that he meant Mia. "Only a few moments before. She was our waitress this morning, for Felix and me. We ate, then Alex arrived. Mia took his order, but when his food came, it was Annie who brought it, not Mia." I'd had plenty of time to go over everything in my mind while we waited.

"So it was just you and Mr. Norcutt in the dining room after that?"

"No, Paul arrived when Felix left."

"How long would you say it was between the time when you saw Ms. Warren in the dining room and you heard Mrs. Bell scream?"

"I have no idea."

"Just an estimate. A guess."

I shrugged. "Maybe five minutes, but I'm not sure at all."

"And had you met Mia Warren before yesterday?"

"No."

Byron nodded. "Thank you Ms. Sharp." It was a dismissal.

"One other thing that I think you should know," I said, hesitantly. "You know that Mia worked in the Pump Room?" He nodded, and I plowed on. During the time while I was waiting and thinking, I'd decided it was something he should know. "After you interviewed me yesterday at the Baths, I went into the Pump Room. That's where our group was set to meet. I recognized Mia and stopped to talk to her. She was interested in Cyrus and asked lots of questions about his death."

"That's natural."

"Yes, I realize that, but she told me she'd talked to him. She said Annie likes for the staff to talk to the guests. She said he mentioned going to Sydney Gardens and then on to the Circus."

Byron watched me for a moment then said, "Ms.

Warren mentioned the same thing to me when I questioned her yesterday. What do you make of it?"

"Me?"

"You obviously think it's important enough to make sure I knew about it."

"I don't know. It seemed that she had taken quite an… interest in Cyrus. She was a bit dazzled with the television connection, I think, and, well, her death can't *not* be related to his, right? It would be too much of a coincidence, wouldn't it?"

"At this point, we can't assume anything," Byron said and looked over my shoulder and nodded, indicating he was ready for the next person. "Please give your contact details to Detective Sergeant Gadd before you go."

I took the pad of paper and wrote down the address of the cottage in Nether Woodsmoor as well as my cell phone number. As I handed it back to Gadd, Byron said, "Mia Warren worked here. Cyrus Blakely was a guest here. Mia's death could be one of those freakishly odd coincidences. Perhaps not. Freakishly odd coincidences are rare in my line of work."

CHAPTER 15

INTERVIEWS COMPLETED, OUR GROUP STOOD on the sidewalk outside the hotel, blinking in the bright sunlight. Byron had finished with us and asked us to stay clear of the hotel until that evening. Official vehicles clogged the street and uniformed officers as well as other investigators traipsed in and out of the hotel.

We stood uncertainly, now on the outside of the crime tape that blocked off the area in front of the hotel. Melissa had left to attend to her mannequins at the Fashion Museum, but the rest of us lingered. Now that we had been dismissed and could go our separate ways, I think we all felt reluctant to break from the group. And there was the fact that the day had a surreal quality to it. It couldn't really have happened—it was too awful.

I ran my gaze around the ring of faces. We all looked a bit shell-shocked. Much more than we had after Cyrus's death. Even though none of us had known Mia personally, it had impacted us more. Was it because it was the second death in as many days? The mind and body can only take so many shocks. Or was it because her death had been more...gruesome? There wasn't another word to describe the blood.

"What now?" Paul asked, interrupting my thoughts.

We all looked toward Elise, but she shrugged. She'd been so brilliant and efficient earlier, but the shock must have caught up with her because she looked almost numb. "I have no idea," she said, quietly.

A man carrying several large bags walked up to the crime tape beside us and looked at the hotel. "Now how is a bloke supposed to get in there?"

Paul said, "Elise, I think this is the lunch delivery."

"Lunch?" Elise asked, absently.

"For the picnic. To Box Hill. We planned it for this afternoon."

She blinked. "I'd forgotten. With everything..." she waved vaguely toward the police vehicles.

"Elise DuPont?" The man asked, consulting a tag clipped to one of the bags.

"Yes, that's me, but I'm afraid—"

"I can see you've had some sort of trouble." He tilted his head toward the crime tape. "But no worries. It's all paid for. I'll leave it here with you." He held out the bags to Paul, obviously identifying Paul as the one who did the grunt work. The man nodded and left.

"Well, I don't know what we're going to do with that," Elise said, a faint trace of her usual vinegar-like personality showing through.

After a long moment, Felix, juggling the change in his pocket, said, "We could go."

"On a picnic? Today?" Elise said, slipping back into uncertainty. "I don't know. It doesn't seem appropriate."

"We have nothing else to do," Felix said. "They won't let us back in until they're done, which could be hours. Might as well carry on as best we can."

"I suppose you're right." She looked around the group. "Any objections?"

"Not from me," I said. "A trip to the countryside might do us all some good."

I glanced at Alex and he nodded. "I'm for it. Let's put some distance between us and Bath, if only for a few hours."

Paul handed off the bags to Elise. "I'll get the van."

A little over two hours later, we arrived at Box Hill and surveyed the gently rolling countryside with its pattern of smooth fields bounded with tufts of hedges, which contrasted with the forested hills and swaying grass of the meadows. Overhead, the sky stretched blue and unmarred by a single cloud. A few picnics were in progress, but it wasn't incredibly crowded.

We all set to work, leaving the food for later. Felix, Elise, and Paul debated the possible angles that would be required to keep the city of Dorking, which sprawled below us, out of the shots. Alex and I photographed, shot some video on our phones, and made notes, even jotting little handmade maps of the area.

I think we were all glad to do some actual work and when we finally found a nice spot in a meadow to settle down with the food, the conversation was still about the pros and cons of the location.

"The angles will be so restricted," Felix said, unwrapping a sandwich.

The bright sunshine made that day almost warm, and Elise had taken off her cloak, which Annie had returned to her before we left the hotel. Elise picked up an apple and gestured to the view. "But we have the opportunity to film at an actual location that Austen wrote about. So many of her locations were fictional, which forces us to improvise. And we *can* film here, unlike Beechen Cliff," Elise said, naming the walk that Catherine takes with Mr. Tilney and his sister in *Northanger Abbey*.

Beechen Cliff was a real place, a hike that gave a great view of the city of Bath, but it was impossible to film there and get the deserted feeling of a country walk because the noise and activity of modern Bath intruded. The beeping noise of buses, or coaches, as they backed up at the bus station directly below, carried up to the cliff, and the train station was also nearby. The subject of filming at Beechen Cliff had come up during our early morning drive to Bath. We'd already discussed the disadvantages of that location and eliminated it from our list of possibilities.

"I think we should take advantage of the authenticity here." Elise had been silent on the drive—we all had, in fact—but now that we were back in our work sphere she'd shaken off the hesitant manner and was back to her old self. "It's not perfect, but it is workable."

Alex and I had spread our coats on the grass for our makeshift picnic blanket. We were a few feet away from Elise, Felix, and Paul. Alex, who had collected our sandwiches, handed one to me and sat down beside me. I said in a low tone, "I wonder how long until the topic of alibis comes up."

"Not long, I imagine."

Felix said, "I still think we should at least look into other locations. This is a tourist spot. Imagine what it will look like in a few months."

"We'll work that out with the locals," Elise said with a glance at Alex and me. I made a note in my Moleskine journal. No matter how much Felix argued, I could tell Elise was set on this location.

Felix shrugged and shifted so that he was facing the view as he ate his sandwich. I had a feeling he was going through the motions of being contrary. His heart didn't seem to be in his arguments.

I was sure our picnic was much less elaborate than any Regency picnic. Austen didn't go into great detail describing the preparations for the Box Hill picnic in *Emma,* but I thought it probably involved lots of servants. No horses toiling uphill pulling wagons of china and silver for us. Only sandwiches and soda, but I doubted any of us wanted a big spread of food right now. We lapsed into silence as we ate. I soaked up the view, letting the greens and browns of the landscape along with the varying textures of trees, meadow, and grass soothe me.

"I wonder where Dominic went?" Elise asked suddenly.

Despite the fact that we hadn't spoken about Mia's death for a while, it was still at the forefront of everyone's mind, because Felix said immediately, "He went to get light bulbs."

"And you know this how?" Elise asked, eyebrows raised.

"I heard him. I was on my way up to my room after

breakfast. As I passed through the kitchen, he said something to Annie about the light on the stairs being out. He said he'd pop out and get a replacement."

Elise said, "I see. I was upstairs when I heard Annie scream." She shivered. "I had no idea what had happened. No one else was by the entry area?"

Alex said, "Kate and I were in the dining room with Paul."

"And Melissa was still upstairs," I said.

Elise frowned. "Hmm…well, at least none of us are suspects in this case. Because whoever killed Mia would have to be covered in blood. Even though the police were trying to keep us away, I saw enough of the office to know that."

Alex opened his mouth to say something, but Felix was a little quicker. "I don't know about that," Felix said. "My interview with Byron did not feel like a routine chat."

I looked at Alex as I chewed a bite of my sandwich, expecting him to speak, but he'd fallen silent. I swallowed and turned back to Felix. "What *did* Byron ask you?"

Felix stared at the patchwork of fields and trees in the distance. "Mostly, he wanted to know about my movements and if I knew Mia before we came here."

"All perfectly normal. He asked me the same thing," Elise said, briskly.

Felix squinted and shook his head. "It wasn't the questions themselves. Something about the way he asked and listened…like he was memorizing every word I said, and later he'd pull them out and examine them one by one. It didn't seem run-of-the-mill to me."

"Heightened awareness from the shock of the death,"

Elise diagnosed in a dismissive tone. She looked toward Paul, "I suppose the only bright side about this whole thing is that you now have an alibi."

Alex and I exchanged a glance.

"For Mia's death," Paul said. "But I doubt the police would give me a passing glance there."

Elise said, "But Mia's death is connected to Cyrus's. It *must* be."

A thought stirred. "Did Byron ask you all for your contact details today?" I asked.

Elise said yes, and everyone else nodded.

"And you wrote them down for him, on the pad of paper?"

Again, nods all around.

"What are you getting at?" Elise asked.

"Just a thought." I wiggled my bottle of water firmly into the grass so that it wouldn't tip over. "I'm not sure what it means, if anything. If it does mean something... well, I suppose we'll find out soon enough."

Elise rolled her eyes.

Felix deposited his empty sandwich wrapper back in the shopping bag. "We should leave soon. The roads will be clogged if we wait much longer."

Elise waved away his concern. "Yes, soon."

I stood. "I think I'll wander around a bit before we go."

"I'll join you," Alex said. We set off across the meadow toward a line of trees.

After we'd walked several paces, Alex asked, "So, are you going to let me in on it?"

"On what?"

"Whatever you're frowning over. Something to do with the contact information?"

I stepped over a tree root. "There may be some completely innocuous reason for it, but Byron already had all our contact information. I gave him mine yesterday. You gave your contact info to him during your interview at the police station, right?"

"Yes."

"So why ask for it again?"

"Bureaucratic incompetence is a possibility."

"Yes, there is that. But he asked each of us to write down the information that we'd already given. Just now, as I was thinking about it, it reminded me of an Agatha Christie novel, *Murder on the Orient Express*," I looked away from the ground to him.

"I'm not a huge mystery reader, but I have heard of that one."

"Just checking," I said, returning his slight smile. "Anyway, Poirot has each suspect write down something for him so he can get a sample of their handwriting."

We walked several paces, and I said, "So, if there's not some computer glitch or mix-up of files that left him without our contact information, why would he want to see what our handwriting looks like?"

We had been walking through an area with a few scattered trees and bushes, but we had reached a thick belt of trees and stepped into their shade. The temperature immediately dropped several degrees. Alex said, "Blackmail is one possibility, I suppose."

"That's what is running around in my mind. You remember how interested Mia was in Cyrus's death, how many questions she asked at the Pump Room. What if she discovered something...something incriminating and threatened to expose the person? But if that is what happened, the blackmail note would be in Mia's handwriting...so why would Byron want handwriting samples from the rest of us?"

"Unless the killer wrote something down...maybe something to lure Mia to the office," Alex said slowly.

We followed a little trail through the trees, the sunlight dappling our shoulders. "And then left the note for the police to find? That's...sloppy," I said.

"Maybe the killer intended to destroy the note, but didn't have time." The path began to climb. As we worked our way up it, taking long vertical steps, Alex said, "Of course, that's all speculation. A computer glitch or delay is probably the most likely explanation of why he wanted our details written down. Maybe he likes to have a paper backup of information."

Alex reached back, and I gripped his hand as we went over a steep section. "Byron didn't strike me as that type of person. He didn't write anything down when he interviewed me."

"Me either." Alex said. "So maybe the handwriting samples do have something to do with blackmail. Mia did work in both places, the hotel and the Pump Room. And the Pump Room is connected to the Baths, which you pointed out to me. She might have been in a position to notice something."

"If the crimes are connected—if the same person killed both Cyrus and Mia—then that means that you, me, and Paul do have alibis," I said.

"Elise will be so relieved," Alex said with a half laugh. "She can mark a couple of names off her spreadsheet."

"Not her own, though," I said. "Interesting that she was so helpful this morning and then sort of fell apart after the police arrived."

The path flattened, and we meandered along it, enjoying the easier walk after the climb.

"Crisis does that to some people," Alex said. "Brings out the best in them, then the reaction sets in later."

"Hmm. I have to say it was one of the few times that she put her bossiness to good use."

Our steps slowed as we came to a point where a fallen tree blocked the path. I stopped and looked back the way we'd come. "We'd better not go too far. Elise might be ready to pack up." I perched on the trunk of the fallen tree.

"Felix seemed like the one who was anxious to leave." Alex sat down beside me. "I see one problem with the handwriting issue. In this day of email and text, why would a millennial like Mia send a handwritten blackmail note?"

"I don't know," I admitted. "Maybe she was smart enough to realize that a text or email could be traced back to her if she sent it over her phone or from her computer."

"That is the sticky issue with blackmail. A clever person might be able to turn the tables."

"As long as they don't care about their secret coming out," I said. "To expose the blackmailer would mean revealing what you're being blackmailed about. And I have to say that I think murder would be something you'd want to hide."

"And possibly murder again to keep hidden," Alex added.

We sat in silence for a few moments.

My thoughts circled back to Elise's alibi theories. "Earlier, you were going to say something when Elise said that whoever killed Mia would have to be covered in blood."

Alex shifted. "I don't think she's right about that. You're the mystery reader, but I don't think it is a given that the killer would be drenched in blood. The walls of the office facing away from the door had blood on them, but the other walls didn't. I noticed that when I left the office—after I realized that there was nothing I could do to help Mia." He picked up a fallen leaf. It was dry and brittle and the color of mud. He twirled the stem between his fingers then said, "Mia must have been in the center of the office, facing away from the door. If the killer stood behind her, he'd probably have blood on his hand, maybe his arm."

"Annie had blood on her hand," I said.

Alex nodded. "Yes. That's what I was thinking about earlier when Elise said what she did. Most of the blood on the walls of the office was on the walls opposite the door, but there was one other place that had blood on it—the light switch. If the killer hit the lights on the way out, it would smear blood all over the switch plate and probably get some on the wall around it. But that was the only place that had any blood on it on that side of the room. Nothing else on that wall or anywhere else near the door had blood, except the light switch."

"So Annie reached in to turn on the light and got blood on her hand that way. I wonder if Annie is left- or right-handed? I don't think I've seen her write anything, but I know it was her left hand that was bloody."

"I don't know which hand she uses," Alex said, "but I

suppose she would use whichever hand was free since she was maneuvering with one crutch today."

"Her right leg is in the cast so she has to hold the crutch with her right hand. She could have reached across and switched on the light with her left hand because it was her free hand."

"Yes. At least, that's what I think happened."

I thought back. "The coating of blood on her left hand was thin. Not like...well, you know what I'm thinking."

He nodded and dropped the leaf. "More like it had been transferred there rather than had blood gush over it."

I watched a leaf fall to the ground then said, "So if Annie was simply unlucky enough to be the first one on the scene, and Dominic was out at the store, then that leaves a very short suspect list for both deaths—Elise and Felix. Oh, and Melissa."

"As long as the deaths are linked and the same person killed both Cyrus and Mia," Alex said. "And it does seem unlikely that two murderers would happen so close together, time-wise, and within the loosely connected group of people at the hotel. Did Melissa have any reason to do away with Cyrus? Or the opportunity?"

"She said he was awful to Paul, but she didn't know about it until last night, so I'd say no. But I'm sure Byron will follow up and verify that she was at the Fashion Museum all day yesterday."

A piercing whistle sounded, and Alex stood. "I believe I hear Elise's melodious tones."

"I just hope Melissa didn't take a long, solitary lunch yesterday," I said as we made our way back through the trees.

CHAPTER 16

IT WASN'T ELISE WHO WAS ready to go; it was Felix. He rounded us up and herded us all into the van like a sheep dog. The drive back was as quiet as the drive out had been, but Felix was right about the traffic, which slowed us down. We didn't get back until it was well after six.

Paul dropped us at the end of the pedestrian walkway and went to park the van. The police vehicles were gone, and the only trace of their presence inside the quiet hotel was crime tape sealing off the doorway and window to the little office.

The hotel seemed unnaturally still. As we moved through the parlor, Annie came out of the kitchen. She looked pale and, unlike her normal quick pace, she moved slowly on her crutch as she crossed the room to us. "The police are finished here…for now. I suppose they'll be back, but they said you're free to return to your rooms. We can go on as normal with serving meals and using this portion of the hotel," she said with a lift of the hand that encompassed the parlor, bar, kitchen, and dining room.

The faint clink of silverware sounded as someone moved in the kitchen, then Dominic appeared, wiping his hands on a towel.

Elise glanced from one of them to the other, then said, "Would you like for us to clear out? I'm sure we could find another hotel."

I almost did a double-take, but managed to refrain myself. It wasn't like Elise to think of other people.

"On a Friday near a holiday?" Annie said, referring to Guy Fawkes Night, the holiday celebrating the discovery of a plot to blow up Parliament in the 1600s. The actual day of the celebration had fallen in the middle of the week, but I'd seen a couple of advertisements for official celebrations with fireworks displays that would take place over the weekend, beginning tomorrow.

"Everything will be full up." Annie shook her head. "No, you must stay. It will help—I think." She paused and blinked, looking away out the window to the street. "Having you here will give me some normal things to do. I need normal at the moment."

"Yes, please do stay," Dominic added in his normal hearty tones as he put his arm lightly around Annie's shoulders. While Annie still had a slightly shell-shocked look about her, Dominic looked like his normal self, as if Mia's death hadn't impacted him at all. Only his frequent, quick glances at Annie showed that anything was wrong. She shifted away and ran the back of her hand along her lashes.

"Well, since you feel that way," Elise said, "we'd be

happy to stay. I'm sure we all have plans for tonight and won't bother you," she added running her gaze around the group.

"I'm dining with a friend," Felix said. "If you'll excuse me…" He skirted around Dominic and Annie and went up the stairs.

Alex looked at me and said, "We have dinner plans as well."

After the group dinner last night, Alex and I had planned to go out as a couple tonight. "Yes. I won't be a moment." I went upstairs and dumped my tote bag on the bed as I looked around the room, but I didn't see any evidence that anyone from the police had been inside the room and searched our belongings. I changed into a warm sweater.

When I came back down a little later, I found Alex sitting in one of the club chairs, staring out the window. "Where is everyone?" I asked.

"Cleared out. Felix came down looking spiffy and nearly jogged out of here."

"Felix? Spiffy?" The two words didn't go together.

"Suit and tie and cologne."

"That's…unusual."

"And Elise told Paul they were having a working dinner, poor guy. They left right after. Is Melissa around?"

I shook my head. "No sign that she's been back."

Her side of the room had looked as if a small tornado had ripped through, flinging clothes, makeup, and shoes in every direction. Melissa was like Alex, who thrived in domestic chaos. It made me twitchy. I was an organized person and liked to have each thing in its place. I'd ignored

Melissa's mess and focused instead on changing into a black sweater with gray pants and boots for dinner. This time of year the sun set in late afternoon. After the warmth and sunshine of the afternoon, the evening had turned cold quickly. "She's probably working overtime to make up for this morning. The preview party is tomorrow night."

"That's right. I'd forgotten."

Tomorrow, Saturday, was to have been the last scheduled day of our scouting trip. The plan had been for our group to attend the preview party for the exhibit at the Fashion Museum with Elise doing some heavy-duty schmoozing with the influential people. Melissa had arranged tickets for us. I'd looked forward to it because the Fashion Museum was part of the building that held Bath's famous Assembly Rooms, where Austen had often attended dances and other society events. But Cyrus's death and now Mia's had pushed all thoughts of galas and parties to the back of my mind. Only the fact that Melissa had left two tickets to the party on my bed upstairs had brought it back to the forefront of my thoughts.

"Ready to scrounge for a table?" Alex asked, extending his arm. We didn't have reservations anywhere, which we'd learned last night were recommended when Bath was full of tourists. That was one reason we ended up at the pub. Elise couldn't get us a table large enough anywhere else.

I slipped my hand through the crook of his elbow. "Let's give it a shot. There's always O'Toole's as a last resort."

We found a little Italian place tucked away near the theater and managed to snag a table for two that was wedged into a corner near the front window. There was barely enough room for us to squeeze into our chairs, but we were glad to get it. We ordered a Margherita pizza and watched the parade of people on the other side of the glass hurrying to make the first show.

By unspoken agreement, we avoided the subject of Cyrus and Mia throughout dinner. It was only afterward as we strolled through Bath that I brought it up again. "I wonder how long we'll have to stay here in Bath? Byron wanted us to stay for Cyrus's inquest, and I'm sure he'll want us to stay for Mia's as well."

"Since we haven't done much actual location scouting it might be a good thing if we extend for a few more days," Alex said. "We haven't checked any hotels."

A big part of planning location shoots involved figuring out where to put everyone when the actual shooting wasn't going on. We needed hotels near enough to the location that transportation wouldn't be a problem as well as hotels that had plenty of single room accommodations with en suite facilities. And then there were the two important requirements that were sort of at odds with each other—a quiet location so that the crew could sleep at odd hours, and extended hours for the bar and room service. "Yes, that has been completely wiped off the agenda—"

We were walking along George Street, the busy street that crossed Milsom Street when I slowed outside a steakhouse as a familiar face caught my eye. The windows ran along George Street, and I had a good view of the first few rows of tables.

"Hey, isn't that Felix?" I tilted my head toward a table for two. "I think it's him, but he looks so different." His hair, instead of falling over his face and poking out at odd angles around his ears and collar, was combed back from his prominent brow, which made him look much more presentable. But there was more to the change than just a physical aspect. He leaned forward over the table as if he didn't want to miss a single word the woman across from him said. He looked slightly dazed as well—as if he was looking at a bright light that had blinded him.

"And he's not alone," Alex said. "No wonder he sprinted out of the hotel. He had a dinner date."

"He *does* look spiffy. Is his shirt actually ironed? And his tie isn't even crooked."

Felix's companion, a woman in a rose-colored dress, was seated facing away from the window so all I could see was the back of her blond head and one hand, which held a glass of white wine. She laughed at something Felix said then turned to the waiter with a smile still on her face as he approached the table.

"That's Octavia," I said.

"Cyrus's widow?"

"His merry widow, by the looks of it."

"OH, and you'll never guess who Alex and I saw on a date tonight," I said to Melissa later that night. I was already in bed reading when she stumbled in at nearly one in the morning. I had tried to sleep, but my mind had continued to spin, running through the events of the last two days. After an hour or so, I'd given up and delved into Agatha Christie's *Peril at End House* on my e-reader.

Melissa had staggered through the door, this time not because of alcohol but because of exhaustion. "We're so close," she had said, talking about the exhibit at the Fashion Museum. "Only a few finishing touches left for tomorrow."

She was now banging about in the bathroom, but when I mentioned seeing someone on a date, all noises stopped abruptly.

"Who? Paul?" she asked with forced casualness.

I grimaced. I'd wondered if I'd possibly misread her last night, thinking that perhaps I was wrong, and she didn't have a bad case of unrequited love directed at Paul. This morning, the few times I'd looked toward her while we waited to be questioned by the police, she'd hardly glanced at Paul and had only said a general goodbye to us all before rushing off to work on the exhibit when we were dismissed. Her seemingly careless tone told me I was wrong. I said quickly, "No, you'll never guess. Felix."

Her head popped around the doorframe of the bathroom. "Felix?" she asked in disbelief.

"Yes with Cyrus's wife, Octavia. Or widow, I mean." I brought her up-to-date on what I'd seen in the Royal Crescent Hotel because she hadn't been there when I told the scouting crew about it. By the time I finished, she was clicking off the bathroom light.

Melissa presented a hard shell to the world, and I tended to think of her as tough and scrappy, but with her face scrubbed clean of her heavy eyeliner and her eyebrow rings removed, she looked uncharacteristically vulnerable.

She crawled into her single bed with a sigh and fell back against the pillow. "I don't suppose that's so weird… not the part about going out on a date on the day after your husband is killed, if they lived separate lives. But that she'd go with *Felix*. He's just not what comes to mind when you think of boyfriend material, is he?" she said with a laugh.

"No. Definitely not."

"But, then again..." she frowned at the ceiling, "...now that I think about it, he is an old friend of her's. More than a friend actually."

"Really?" I put down my e-reader.

Melissa rolled onto her side. "Yeah, Octavia and Felix go way back. I forget who was talking about it. I mentioned Cyrus to..." she yawned, "...someone...oh, it was Patty in Post Production. This was a few months ago. Patty always knows all the gossip—and can't wait to share it. Anyway, she said that Octavia and Felix were quite the item at one time...engaged, in fact."

"Wow, he's certainly been cagey about that. Not a word about it."

"Can't say that I blame him. Octavia broke it off with Felix once she met Cyrus."

"Ah. I wouldn't want to talk about something like that either."

"Yeah, apparently it was no secret. Patty was around then. She said everyone knew that Felix was loopy about Octavia, but then Cyrus came along." Melissa snuggled deeper under the covers. "Once Cyrus was on the scene, Octavia dropped Felix."

"How sad," I said, thinking of Felix's expression that I'd seen tonight through the window. He'd looked eager and slightly dazed at the same time.

"He had money. Cyrus, I mean. Felix was stony broke. Cyrus came from old money. Upper crust education. Old family pile in the country, but unlike so many of those blokes, Cyrus's family actually has money. Must be investments or something. So it was goodbye Felix, hello Cyrus." Melissa scowled. "Can you imagine freely picking Cyrus as a husband? Not that I think Felix is a prize or anything. I mean, they're both so old, but at least Felix isn't a pompous twit." She yawned again and rolled over.

I sat thinking about what she'd said, all the questions still swirling in my mind, which brought me back to the issue of alibis. "Hey, Melissa," I said softly. "Are you still awake?"

"Hmm," she murmured without rolling over.

"Were you at the Fashion Museum all day yesterday?"

"Yeah."

"You didn't take a long lunch or anything like that?"

"Are you kidding? We worked non-stop all day, and we still have stuff left to do. Marie even had sandwiches brought in for lunch so we could work straight through."

"Okay, that's good."

I expected her to ask why I wanted to know, but she only readjusted her pillow. After a few seconds I could tell from her breathing that she had fallen asleep almost immediately.

It was a long time before I slept.

CHAPTER 17

ELISE HADN'T SET A TIME for us to meet the next morning, but by eight we were all in the dining room. Breakfast was a somber affair with Annie and Dominic working in complete silence as they moved back and forth from the kitchen to the dining room, serving our food and distributing coffees to the locals who dropped in for their morning caffeine hit. Mia must have been their only other employee because no one else helped them with the food. Annie looked more haggard than she had the day before. She leaned heavily on her crutch as she worked. Dominic did most of the work, swiftly delivering plates, refilling coffee and teapots, and then swooping empty plates away.

Melissa grabbed a croissant. "Must dash. Loads of last minute details. I'll see you all tonight."

Annie, who had just refilled the juicer with fresh oranges stopped, the empty basket pressed into the side of her body that wasn't leaning on the crutch. "Oh. The preview party. I'd completely forgotten."

"Will you be there?" I asked.

Dominic splashed a refill of coffee into my cup. "Of course we'll be there. Annie has her finger in every pie in town, I think."

The words themselves weren't mean, but his tone was disparaging. Annie's mouth flattened into a line. "It's important to support what we can. No one would come to visit Bath if there was nothing to do here."

"I doubt the Roman Baths will turn to dust if you're not personally involved in every fundraising effort," Dominic said. "They've moldered on for thousands of years without you. Same thing with the Fashion Museum."

Annie seemed to shrink a bit at his words. "Nevertheless, we are committed for tonight." She gripped her crutch and thumped slowly into the kitchen where a delivery had arrived.

Dominic threw us all a rueful smile. "Annie and her causes. It's always something." He followed her into the kitchen. Over the clatter of dishes and rush of water I heard Annie's voice as she said sharply, "If you don't want to go, stay home. I'm going. I should be there to support Marie."

"Ah, support." Dominic's deep voice with its sarcastic tone carried into the dining room. "The magic word. We must support this or that. Why? It doesn't matter if we show up tonight or not. It won't make one bit of difference."

The sound of running water drowned out their voices. Elise cleared her throat. "Our itinerary has been thrown off rather radically, so today it's important that we get several things accomplished. Alex and Kate, you check these hotels." She handed a list to Alex. "Paul and I will take this second list," she said, nodding to the paper that Paul held. She glanced toward the kitchen where the low angry conversation continued. "Felix, by my calculations, you and I are the only ones left who need an alibi. As we discussed yesterday, I'm sure the two deaths are linked. Since Paul, Kate, and Alex were together when Mia's death occurred, I'm sure the Byron will consider them in the clear for Cyrus's murder as well. After Paul and I check the hotels on our list, I'll try to firm up my alibi for the time Cyrus was killed. Paul, I expect you to do the same. Pity neither of us came down a bit earlier yesterday."

I wasn't sure that Byron would fall in with Elise's confident assertions, but I was glad she'd slightly backed off her alibi hobbyhorse. I was all for doing some location scouting. It would be good to delve into work.

Elise checked her watch. "The preview party begins at seven. We will all attend," she said in a tone that meant there would be no debate about the subject. She stood. "You all have received your tickets? Good. I will see you then."

ALEX and I spent the day visiting hotels. We stood still in guest rooms as we listened for street noise, and toured the various amenities of the properties—pools, spas, bars, restaurants and less glamorous features like parking garages. By the time four o'clock rolled around, we had two hotels left. "Better split up," Alex said, "since they are on opposite sides of town."

"Sounds good. That will give us time to get back to the hotel, change, and grab some dinner before the preview party."

"Change? Why would we need to change?" Alex asked.

"It's formal…not black tie or anything, but you have to dress up. You brought a suit jacket, right? You do own a suit jacket, don't you?" Alex's style was casual, running along the lines of jeans rather than suits.

He grinned suddenly. "I had you going there. Of course, I own a suit jacket. My father is in the diplomatic service. I know how to dress for the occasion. See you at the hotel."

We parted, and I made my way over Pulteney Bridge to Laura Place, thinking of Lady Dalrymple and *Persuasion*. I stopped to take in the exterior of what was once the Sydney Hotel, but is now a museum, wishing I had more time and could tour the building. Sydney Gardens was beyond the museum, but I didn't have time to stop there. Sydney Gardens also made me think of Cyrus, and I wondered if there was a way to find out where he'd gone in the Gardens. I didn't have time to check into it, and surely Byron was pursuing that question.

I found the hotel, but a quick tour showed me that it wouldn't be a good fit. There were plenty of rooms and they were quiet, but only a few of them were singles. I marked it off the list and headed back to the hotel along Great Pulteney Street. Before I reached the bridge, I trotted down a set of stone steps for a quick detour, following a sign to the riverside walk.

I made my way through a little park area for a closer

look at the Avon, the river that partially encircled Bath. I paused at a viewing point near the water and leaned on an iron railing. When I looked back at Pulteney Bridge, the reflection of the arched bridge supports in the water created the illusion of complete stone circles. The water flowed flat and smooth under the bridge, then rushed over the Weir, a series of stepping-stone-like curves below the bridge. The curves were designed in an oval shape, which I thought was appropriate for Bath because so many of its architectural features were circles, crescents, and curves.

After taking several pictures, I pushed away from the railing and retraced my steps, then climbed back to the street. As I crossed Pulteney Bridge, I glanced in the shops that lined it. I moved around a pair of women admiring a display of necklaces in the window of a jeweler, then stopped as a couple stepped out of the store directly into my path.

"Excuse—oh, Kate," Alex said.

"Hi," I said, glad that we'd met up again. "I thought you were over near Camden Crescent…oh, hi, Viv."

"I was," Alex said, "but the last hotel was a washout. I finished early."

"Me too."

Alex shifted his feet and darted a glance from Viv to me, not looking at all like his usual relaxed and easy-going self. In fact, I realized, he definitely looked uncomfortable as he said, "I was heading your way—"

"When I saw him." Viv bounced on her toes. "The bike shop where I work is only a few blocks away. I saw him come in here and had to pop over and say hello." Today she wore a slouchy large weave sweater over a pair of black leggings with running shoes. Some of her long auburn hair was tucked under a knit beanie, but most of it trailed around her shoulders. Viv smiled and shot a glance at Alex. "I managed to catch up and join him for a bit of shopping." She placed an extra emphasis on the last word, and her eyes sparkled with an I've-got-a-secret vibe.

What was it with Viv showing up everywhere we were —correction, everywhere Alex was? And that special smile she was flashing at Alex—I took a breath when I noticed Alex's face. I knew that look. Polite on the surface, but underneath, he was irritated. I'd seen that look often enough when we were bogged down with work and someone wasn't pulling their weight. He was annoyed—and it wasn't with me. I made an effort to not let the exasperation I felt with Viv show on my face. It was childish, this selfish desire to wish she was far away from Alex.

"I thought I'd swing by and see if you were still around here," Alex said to me.

"I went down to see the river."

"Oh, sorry I missed that. I'd like to see it, too," Alex said.

"I don't think there's time now," I said. "With the…ah… plans we have for tonight." I held back from mentioning the preview party, afraid that if I said something about it, Viv would want to tag along there, too. It was an entirely selfish thought, but I couldn't help it. Her bright smile and the way she constantly focused on Alex's face irked me.

"Right," Alex said, reaching out to take my hand. "We have to go. See you around, Viv."

"Okay. Sure. I'm at the bike shop again tomorrow after lunch. I'd love for you to drop in," she called at our retreating backs. "Anytime would be great."

Alex waved and gave her a half smile, but kept up his quick pace. When we reached an arcaded shopping area, he glanced back over his shoulder and slowed down. "I was walking along the street, on my way to look for you, and the next thing I knew she was in the street behind me, calling my name. She said she was on her dinner break and would walk with me. I couldn't get rid of her."

"Alex, you don't have to explain." We worked our way through a knot of tourists gathered outside the Roman Baths and the Pump Room.

"I don't know what's up with her," Alex said.

I thought I knew exactly what was up with her, but I kept that thought to myself. As we neared the turn for the street with our hotel, we slowed our steps. Two policemen stood beside a small area that was blocked off. Police tape had been stretched around two barriers, creating a square. I couldn't see much inside the square, except that an iron grate had been removed from the street. One man in a hard hat leaned over the opening, sweeping a flashlight back and forth.

As we turned down the pedestrian walkway to go to the hotel, Alex said, "Viv wasn't like this when I knew her before."

He looked so rattled, and, secure in the knowledge that he didn't want Viv's attention, I couldn't help poking a little fun at him. "Maybe she's stalking you."

"That's probably going a *little* far," he said. "But she does keep turning up."

"Like a bad penny," I said and by then we'd reached the hotel.

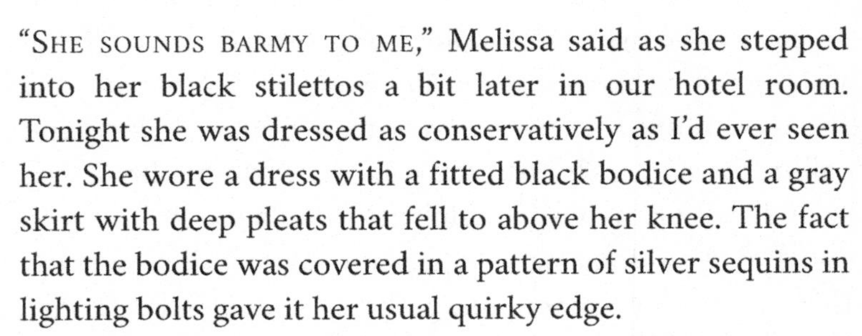

"She sounds barmy to me," Melissa said as she stepped into her black stilettos a bit later in our hotel room. Tonight she was dressed as conservatively as I'd ever seen her. She wore a dress with a fitted black bodice and a gray skirt with deep pleats that fell to above her knee. The fact that the bodice was covered in a pattern of silver sequins in lighting bolts gave it her usual quirky edge.

I hunched over the vanity, adding an extra layer of mascara. "I don't know if I'd go that far. Aggressive, I'd say."

"That, too." Melissa picked up her beaded purse. "Look, Alex is a sweet guy and all, but he *is* a guy. You might have to make it clear to her that he's off the market."

I screwed the mascara wand back into the tube and tossed it in my makeup bag. "That would be going too far, I think."

"I'm telling you, girls like that don't play by the rules. She's obviously making a play for Alex. I know he's crazy about you and all," she brushed aside my protest. "Yes, he is. Anyone who looks at you two together can see it, *but* when a girl like Viv is on the prowl, you can't be too polite."

I shook my head. "I'm not going to do that."

"Why not? I've seen you fix problems like that on the set," she said with a snap of her fingers.

"Because this is different. That's work. This is...personal."

"So you're going to sit back and just trust Alex."

I thought about it for a second and realized there was only one answer to the question. Despite our time apart and the initial bumpiness of being back together, deep down I didn't doubt him. "Yes. I do trust Alex."

Melissa's combative stance dropped away. She rolled her eyes to the ceiling and said with a grin, "Okay, now *you're* the barmy one."

CHAPTER 18

"IT MUST BE ALONG HERE somewhere." I looked at the numbers on the doors along the street. Alex and I were laboring up Gay Street, which was one place where Jane Austen had lived in Bath. She actually had several different residences in the city, but Gay Street was on the way to the preview party, and I couldn't resist looking for her house.

Like most streets in Bath, Gay Street was elegant. Three-story terraced houses with mansard roofs and Ionic columns lined each side. Wrought iron railings enclosed staircases that disappeared below ground to basements, the area that would have once been the servant's entrance while the main entrances to the houses were on the street level.

Earlier, I had met Alex in the hotel's parlor and was relieved to see that his easy manner had returned. He wore a black jacket with a silver gray tie. Melissa would have given a wolf whistle, but I settled for saying, "You do clean up well."

"My embassy training comes through again. You look lovely," he said as he held my gaze, and I wondered why I had wasted a minute of my time worrying about Viv when he looked at me like that. He had offered his arm, and I slipped my hand through his elbow, vowing to be less irritated the next time Viv popped up—as I was sure she would.

We had dined at a restaurant that served huge portions of rotisserie chicken. The subject of Viv didn't come up, but I almost expected to see her peering in the window, hands clasped around her eyes. Thankfully, it was just Alex and me for dinner. No unexpected guests. I was stuffed by the time we finished dinner and wanted to walk off some of the meal before we hit the party with its heavy hors d'oeuvres, so I had suggested we stroll up the street where Austen had once lived.

On our way up the steep street, we'd already passed the Jane Austen Center with its rather intimidating mannequin in Regency costume, which I thought looked more like Fanny Dashwood in Emma Thompson's film version of *Sense and Sensibility* rather than any image of Jane Austen that I'd seen.

"Here it is." I stopped before a door with an iron fence on either side of it. "Number Twenty-Five." I read the gold plaque beside the door. "It's now...a dentist office."

"Rather prosaic."

"I think Austen would find some humor in that situation," I said, and we turned to toil up the rest of the incline to the Assembly Rooms at a quick pace because of the chilly night air. Alex had photographed the Assembly Rooms on our first day in Bath, but I had never seen them.

The exterior resembled a temple from classical times with columns supporting a pediment, but along simpler lines than most temples from antiquity. No frieze ornamented the peak over the entry. As we joined the line at the door, I thought of Austen's description of Catherine Moreland's first visit to the Assembly Rooms, in which their male escort abandoned Catherine and her chaperone for the card room and left them to enjoy "the mob" by themselves. In the book, Catherine and her chaperone fight their way through the press to the top of the room, but still can't see anyone because of the crowd.

By Regency standards, the crowd for the preview party would have been viewed as a tepid turnout—one mark of a successful Regency party was that the event was so crowded you could hardly move through the rooms—but I was glad we didn't have to fight our way inside.

We were swept into the modest tide of people arriving and carried downstairs to the basement floor where the Fashion Museum was located. I caught a quick glimpse of Elise. She wore a cocktail dress—black, of course—but she'd taken time to put actual combs in her hair. It was confined to a tight bun and only a few strands of hair had escaped.

Alex and I meandered around the rooms, marveling at the outrageous court gowns from the Georgian period with their skirts that stuck out sideways from the hips.

"That is just ridiculous," Alex said.

"But the height of fashion in the 1700s," Melissa said, joining us. "Did you have a nice dinner? Anyone drop in on you?" she asked, eyes wide.

Alex glanced at her sharply. I said, "Oh, look at Paul

over there by the wall. Elise has abandoned him while she schmoozes." Paul was also turned out in a suit and tie and was sans pencil tonight. "You should go talk to him," I said to Melissa and gave her a little push in his direction then waved to get Paul's attention. He moved toward her, a relieved look on his face.

Alex said, "Playing matchmaker?"

"Only on a very small scale. Nothing *Emma*-like, I assure you."

Alex grinned. "I've seen the movie, but not read the book, but I do get the allusion."

We moved around the room, checking out the permanent display of Georgian costumes then strolled through the Regency exhibition with its high-waisted fashions for women and cutaway coats for men. "They all look so tiny, don't they?" I said.

"Yes, that's why the talent is always on a diet on set—to fit into clothes like this."

Eventually we moved back up the stairs to the ground floor. The building lacked a grand exterior, but the interior of the rooms more than made up for it. The ballroom was in use for another event, and I only had a glimpse of a row of massive chandeliers and ornate molding on the room's pale blue walls before we moved through an octagon-shaped room into what had been the Tea Room during the Regency.

More Regency clothes were displayed in glass cases arranged around the edges of the spacious room. The Tea Room wasn't as large as the ballroom—it only had three glittering chandeliers—but it was still impressive with a lofty coved ceiling and a colonnaded balcony.

I spotted Annie chatting with a group of people, her crutch leaning on a tall round table beside them, but Dominic wasn't with her. The table next to her came open, and we wandered toward it. Annie gave us a quick smile and lift of her head as she saw us, but she appeared deep in conversation, so we didn't join her.

Somehow Elise had beaten us upstairs and now had another knot of people cornered. "...so you can see how these productions contribute to increased interest in preservation of actual artifacts," Elise said, "not to mention the uptick we see in the historical genres associated with it. When the first episodes ran, we saw an increase of twenty-four percent in visits to..."

"I'm glad my job doesn't involve talking up our project."

Alex said, "Elise may be...ah—challenging, let's say, to work with, but she does whatever is needed to get the job done."

"Spoken like the son of a diplomat," I said lightly, but then turned serious. "She's one of the few people who doesn't have an alibi for either Cyrus or Mia's death," I said uncomfortably. No matter what was happening the two deaths weren't far from my thoughts. "It doesn't matter how much effort she puts into trying to find someone to give her an alibi, you know that Byron has to be looking at her pretty hard."

"Her and Felix." Alex raised his eyebrows, indicating I should look over my shoulder.

"I thought maybe he skipped out." I pivoted and scanned the room. But he was in attendance, looking as polished and well-groomed as he had the night before.

"With someone, too," Alex said as the crowd around

Felix shifted and revealed a blond woman in a beautifully cut pink cocktail dress beside him. "Is that...?"

I had a better vantage point than Alex and could see her face. "Yes. That's Octavia."

"Ah," Alex said. "The woman who tossed him over for a richer man." During our hotel research earlier in the day, I'd told Alex all the details I'd heard from Melissa.

"Much richer, according to Melissa," I said.

Alex said, "Looks like he's still besotted, poor guy."

Felix had that same dazed expression on his face that we'd seen at the restaurant. "I have a feeling he's in for a world of hurt," I said. "You'd think that since she'd dumped him once, he would be more cautious."

Alex covered the back of my hand, which was looped through his elbow. "But not all of us are as cool-headed about love as you are."

I looked at him sharply, but it wasn't a dig. His tone wasn't critical. But there was a trace of...what?...sadness, maybe.

"I'll get us a drink," Alex said. "Can't be at one of these affairs without a glass in your hand. Back in a moment."

I watched his broad shoulders as he moved deftly through the crowd.

"Why the frown?" asked a voice beside me, and I turned to see Felix and Octavia. "No frowning allowed at these events," Felix said. "Or at least, don't let Elise see you looking like that. Happy, happy, happy. We love our job. Best job in the world," he said in a falsely bright voice, then returned to his normal tones. "Can't convince people to support your projects if your workers look like they're going to a funeral." Felix flushed, glanced quickly at

Octavia, and cleared his throat. "Sorry, my dear. Didn't think."

"Don't worry about it." Octavia waved her glass. "It's no use pretending that I'm upset about either Cyrus's death or his funeral. I'm not. I won't be a hypocrite about it."

"This is Kate," Felix said, belatedly. "Location scout with the production. Kate, this is a good friend of mine, Octavia Blakely."

As we shook hands, Octavia said, "So you were under Cyrus's thumb as well? You have my complete sympathy."

"I'd only just met him."

"Lucky you," Octavia said.

Alex returned with our drinks, saving me from coming up with a reply. As introductions were made again, a burly figure moved through my peripheral vision. It was Dominic, dressed in a dark suit, making his way to the table next to us where he joined Annie. Annie smiled at him perfunctorily, and he smiled back just as automatically, but there was no warmth between them.

Felix noticed as well. "So Dominic did show up, despite his grousing."

"Who, darling?" Octavia asked before tilting her glass for a sip.

"Dominic."

Octavia took a long drink, then scanned the room. "Really?" Her voice caught as she spoke. She patted her throat and coughed into a napkin. "Sorry. No, I'm fine. It's been ages since I've seen him. I should say hello." She craned her neck as she scanned the room. "Where is he?"

"Right behind us," Felix said with a tilt of his head. "With Annie."

"Oh." The enthusiasm drained from her tone. "No, they look as if they're in deep conversation. I'll wait."

We talked about the costumes and some of the sites we'd visited around Bath, then the conversation flagged. Finally, Octavia said, "Since you're all involved, I suppose you've heard that the inquest is scheduled for Monday?"

"No," Alex said, speaking for all of us. "We hadn't received word."

"I'm sure Elise decided to keep it back until after the party tonight," Felix said.

I wondered if the police had come to some conclusion about Cyrus's death and about who did it. In mystery fiction, inquests were completed without all the questions being answered, but I wondered if that would be the case here.

"I wonder when Mia's will be?" I said, "I'm sure Byron will want us to stay on here in Bath until after that one as well," I said.

Tiny frown lines appeared under Octavia's fringe of bangs. "Mia?"

"The maid who was killed," I said.

Octavia blinked and the lines became furrows as she raised her eyebrows. "Someone else has been killed? Here? In Bath?"

I glanced from her shocked face to Felix's. He sent me a subtle shake of the head, his face suddenly looking as if his dinner didn't agree with him.

I hesitated, and Octavia shifted her attention to him. "What's this? What's happened?"

Felix swallowed. "She was a maid at the hotel. She was killed yesterday."

Octavia put her glass down carefully. "At the hotel? At *your* hotel?"

"Yes, the Bath Spa Hotel. I should have said something, I realize that now," Felix said, his words rushing out, "but I didn't want to worry you. You have so much—"

"You said she was killed," Octavia said sharply. "That means...how did she die? It wasn't an accident?"

"No," Felix said. "It was—well, her throat was cut. We don't know what happened. There's a chance it's not linked at all to Cyrus's death. It could be random, just some horrible coincidence..." Felix trailed off, looking more miserable. Octavia wasn't looking at him.

"The police didn't contact you?" I asked her, thinking that if they hadn't contacted her it might be a slight confirmation that the crimes weren't linked.

"There was a message today," she said in an uneasy tone as she looked toward Felix, "from that horrible pushy police person. I didn't return his call."

Octavia switched her gaze to the table. Above the decorative beading of her cocktail gown, I could see the pulse at the base of her throat beating rapidly. She was breathing in and out quickly, too. "Are you all right?" I asked, concerned at the abrupt change in her manner. She had gone from carefree and chatty to withdrawn and upset in seconds. "Can I get you some water?"

"No," she said, but she wasn't looking at me. Her gaze swiveled toward Felix. "No, there's nothing you can do."

CHAPTER 19

"I SAW HER FACE," I said. "She was scared."

"She did look shaken," Alex agreed as we walked back to the hotel after the preview party. The restaurants and bars were busy, but the shops had closed, giving Bath a late-night feeling even though it was only a little after nine. We passed the colonnaded entrance to the square in front of the Roman Baths and the Abbey. The surrounding coffee shop and souvenir shop were dark, but the Abbey was brightly lit, a splash of soaring stone in the darkness. We paced on, our footfalls echoing along the cobblestones as we turned onto the street where the hotel was located.

Alex punched in the code to the night latch and pushed the door open. "What's worrying you?"

"So many things," I said as I went through the entry area where crime tape still sealed the reception office. I paused in the parlor. "Octavia was looking at Felix." I instinctively lowered my voice, even though the room was empty. The rest of the hotel was probably empty as well since Annie and Dominic had been at the event along with all of our group.

"I don't understand." Alex loosened his tie. "The news obviously frightened Octavia, but how does Felix come into it...other than being the one person who intentionally kept the news from her?"

"Once she heard the news, she changed—her whole manner."

Alex nodded in agreement. Octavia had left immediately without saying another word. Felix had gone after her, but returned to the room within a minute or two, looking as if his world had fallen apart.

"It's more than she was just generally scared," I said. "She looked at Felix...oh, I don't know how to describe it—frightened and horrified, I guess is the closest I can come to defining it. I think she's afraid *of* him."

Alex said slowly, "So you think, that somehow the news about Mia's death made Octavia think Felix is the murderer?"

"I don't like thinking it. In fact, I hate all this suspicion, wondering if one of our group did it, but," I sighed and said, "he doesn't have an alibi."

"For either death," Alex agreed.

The night latch rattled, then someone pounded on the door. We both moved to the bow window and looked toward the hotel's door. Paul stood in front of it with his phone pressed to his ear, alternately rattling the door handle and pounding on the door with his free hand.

Alex unlocked the door, and Paul hurried inside. "Thanks, mate." He crossed the parlor and looked around. "Hold on, I'm inside now," he said into the phone. "I'll talk to Dominic. He'll know someone…well, at this point you can't be choosy," Paul said, his voice unusually blunt.

Alex and I exchanged a surprised glance. Paul ended the call and peered into the kitchen. "Where's Dominic?"

"I don't think he's here," I said.

"I'll try their living quarters," Paul said over his shoulder as he walked through the bar to a short corridor on the far side of the room. He disappeared from view, but we could hear him as he pounded on a door and called Dominic's name. After a few tries, Paul returned to the parlor, looking completely baffled. "I have no idea what to do. I can't just Google solicitors and pick someone."

"Why do you need a solicitor?" Alex asked.

"Not me. Elise. A bloke came up to her at the party and asked to talk to her privately. She went off with him, and the next thing I know, people were asking for her, and I couldn't find her. But the party was breaking up anyway, so it wasn't critical. I figured she'd gotten tired and headed back here, so I left. When I was about a block away from here, I got a call from her. She's with the police."

The door opened again, and Felix came in, his expression the human equivalent of a basset hound's melancholy face. He didn't say anything, just lifted his chin a few millimeters by way of greeting.

"The man who came to the party and asked for her, was it DCI Byron?" I asked, a bad feeling in my gut.

"No, it wasn't him," Paul said. "I would have recognized him. It was someone else. He was in a suit, but he did have the look of someone with the police."

Felix paused on his way across the room with his hands

in his pockets and his shoulders rounded. "What's happened?" he asked in a disinterested way.

"Apparently Elise has been taken in for questioning," I said. "And she didn't say anything else on the phone?" I asked Paul.

"Oh, she said plenty," Paul said. "She's held them off, saying she'd be happy to answer their questions—something about a glove she lost and both murders being linked—as soon as her solicitor arrives. Then she went and called me," Paul scraped a hand through his hair. "She doesn't have a solicitor—she's delaying, trying to put them off."

"Why would she do that?" I asked.

"Because she's Elise," Paul said. "She's furious with them, and she's not going to give them an inch, but I don't know any solicitors at all, and I especially don't know any solicitors in Bath. That's why I need Dominic."

Felix said, "He and Annie left before I did. They must have stopped off somewhere for a nightcap."

"You know Elise," Paul said, his eyes looking a little wild. "She won't understand that. She wants a solicitor, and she wants one now."

Felix heaved a sigh. "Let me make a call." He took out his cell phone and moved into the bar area.

"So the police are interested in a glove?" I asked with a glance at Alex.

Paul nodded. "Yes, as far as I can tell. She wasn't clear on that point. Something about it had turned up and was causing trouble."

"Didn't she mention that she'd lost her glove the other day?" Alex asked.

"Yes," I said. "We were leaving the pub, I think. She

couldn't find her gloves and said she must have left them in the hotel. Maybe Annie or Dominic saw it somewhere—"

While I was speaking, the door opened again, and Annie made her way across the entry and into the parlor, her crutch swinging slowly. The party must have tired her out, I thought. Dominic followed her in.

"Saw what?" she asked.

"A glove. One of Elise's. It would be black, of course," I said. "She thought she lost it in the hotel."

"Oh, in that case, we should check the lost and fou—" Annie glanced at the entry and the crime scene tape. "Normally, if we find things like that, they go in the lost and found, but it's..." she gestured at the entry area, "...sealed off at the moment. I don't remember seeing any gloves lying around, though."

"Nor do I," Dominic said then added in his usual effusive tones, "Of course, we can find a spare set of mittens, if someone is in desperate need."

Felix's voice, which had been rumbling in the background, fell silent. He rejoined our group as he put his phone away. "That's sorted. Friend of mine lives not too far away from here. He says he'll come in."

"Everything all right?" Dominic asked, his gaze moving from one tense face to another.

"Elise needs a solicitor," Paul said and went on to explain.

Annie looked stricken. "Oh, that's terrible. They don't think—surely it couldn't be her, could it?"

Dominic went quiet. "Elise," he said in a thoughtful manner, which was a contrast to his usual hearty way. He sucked in a breath. "Well, you never know about people."

~

DOMINIC AND ANNIE offered to help in any way possible, but there didn't seem to be much we could do except wait. They offered to bring us hot chocolate or a nightcap, but none of us took them up on the offer. The reality of what was going on had hit us all. If Elise was guilty…of either murder…then the production was done. With the director murdered and the producer accused of murder, the production would fold. We would all be out of work—a trivial thing compared to two lives cut short, but I couldn't help thinking about it. From the subdued air in the parlor, we were all pondering the same thing.

By unspoken agreement we'd all stayed together in the parlor, waiting for news after Dominic and Annie said goodnight and retired to their private living quarters at the back of the hotel. I had dropped into one of the club chairs by the bow window and the rest of the scouting party was scattered around the room. Melissa had to stay after the party to pack away the extra costumes that had been displayed around the Tea Room. She'd told me that those items weren't part of the exhibit and had to be returned to the individuals who had lent them for the party.

She arrived about an hour later and looked delighted to see Paul. He threw her an answering smile, but once we'd told her what had happened, she plopped down on a chair beside me, clearly stunned. "Elise? They think *Elise* murdered Cyrus and Mia?" She shook her head. "I just don't see it."

"Elise and Cyrus didn't get along. We all heard them argue on the drive down here," I said. "And Cyrus opposed practically every single thing Elise wanted to do. With him out of the way…"

"But someone would replace him," Melissa said. "And that's not even taking into account that his death put the whole production in jeopardy."

"If it was a crime of passion she might not have thought it through," Alex said.

"When have you known Elise to be anything but strategic?" Melissa said, looking around the group. "She might not like certain things, but she is practical. Like the thing with Cyrus. She didn't like him. He didn't like her, but she saw that having him on the roster would be a boost to getting the next set of episodes made, so she went with it. It's true, fighting him all the way, but no matter how much Elise despised Cyrus or his 'vision,'" she made a face as she made air quotes, "she wouldn't murder him." She threw a hand out toward Paul. "If anything, she'd delegate the task to Paul."

One corner of his mouth turned up. "That I could *almost* see."

"And what earthly reason would she have to kill Mia?" Melissa asked.

I said, "I suppose that if the police think the crimes are linked…?" I looked toward Paul, eyebrows raised.

He shrugged. "She wasn't quite coherent. She said something about her lost glove and blood and then said something like, 'it's nonsense to think that I—or anyone in our group—would murder both Cyrus and Mia. Utter nonsense to try and link both crimes to us.'"

Melissa leaned back. "I wonder—"

"What is it?" I asked.

"It may be completely unrelated, but earlier this afternoon, I had to rush back here and pick up a set of labels that I'd left here by accident. As I came down the street, some workers were setting up barriers and chatting with a couple of police."

"Alex and I saw them, too."

"Well, I heard them talking. One guy was complaining about having searched every dumpster and wheelie bin in the area and now they were moving on to the drains, looking for a bit of bloodstained cloth." Melissa shrugged. "Maybe they found Elise's glove, and it had blood on it."

"That would explain them wanting to talk to her so late at night," I said.

Melissa tilted her head to the side. "I know I don't read Agatha Christie like you, Kate, but if Elise lost her glove and it was in the hotel's lost and found in the office, then anyone could have slipped it on when they…you know… killed Mia. Then, later they could shove it down the grate in the street."

"That's true," I said slowly, thinking of the wide metal spaces in the grate that had been resting on the ground as the men searched. The spaces were certainly wide enough that a small piece of material, like a glove or scarf could be shoved through. I didn't voice the rest of my thought—if Elise didn't use the glove to protect her from getting blood on her hand, then who did?

My gaze strayed to Felix, who was pacing back and forth in the confines of the bar area. He didn't look good. His skin was pasty. His slicked back appearance—his neatly combed hair and smooth shirt—was disintegrating. He'd run his fingers through his hair, and it now fell forward over his brow. His tie was askew, and his shirt was rumpled. His phone rang, and we all started. He listened for a few moments, then said, "Yes…of course…thank you for letting me know."

"My solicitor friend has arrived. He had a word with both Elise and DCI Byron. He, the solicitor, I mean, says that it will be sometime in the early hours of the morning before anything is resolved and for us to turn in. He'll see that Elise gets back here…if the police release her." He shrugged. "I suppose we should turn in. Tomorrow may be…quite trying. We should all get some rest."

I certainly didn't think I would get a good night's rest, but I couldn't think of anything more productive that I could do. As I stood, the cushion of the club chair shifted, and a paperback book that had been shoved down between the edge of the cushion and the arm of the chair fell to the ground. A square of paper slid out of it.

It was Annie's copy of *Northanger Abbey*. I picked it up along with the paper, which I assumed was a bookmark, automatically glancing at it as I stuck it inside the book. I had a half-formed thought that I'd have to tell Annie tomorrow that I'd knocked her bookmark out of the book, but then the words on the paper registered, completely erasing those thoughts.

I'll tell, if you don't pay.

CHAPTER 20

"KATE?" ALEX'S VOICE SEEMED TO come from a long distance.

I looked up. Everyone was ahead of me, going up the stairs to the rooms, but they had all glanced back at me.

"Are you coming up?" Alex asked, giving me a questioning look.

I shoved the note into the book and tucked it under my arm. "Yes, of course, but I know I won't be able to sleep."

"Neither will I," Melissa said, "but sitting around here won't do Elise any good. We've done all we can for now."

I joined the group and went up the stairs, the book under my arm, my thoughts churning. I'd instinctively hidden the book from everyone's view the second I realized they were watching me, and I kept it hidden as I climbed the stairs.

Contrary to what Melissa said, she took the first round in the bathroom and was snoring by the time I'd changed and washed my face. I'd put the book inside my makeup bag and carried it with me into the bathroom. Now I removed the book and slipped under the covers.

I bent the pages of the book into a curve and fanned them until I reached the page where I'd deposited the note. I studied it without touching it.

It was written on an unlined piece of plain white paper that looked like it had been torn from a notepad. It was about three-inches wide and two-inches long. The writing was in blue ink, the letters slanted and squished together as if the writer had been in a hurry. The top edge was irregular and jagged, and the paper curled a bit on one side.

I stared at the note for quite a few minutes, trying to work out a gender from the handwriting. Unfortunately, it wasn't an obviously feminine hand with graceful loops and curves. Neither was it the careful printing that I had seen some men use. Someone who specialized in handwriting analysis might be able to deduce the writer's sex, but it looked gender neutral to me. The note was still tucked into the spine of the book, and I tilted the pages of the book so that I could see the back of the note, but there wasn't a single squiggle.

It could be Mia's writing. If she had seen what happened...or even worked out who murdered Cyrus on a hunch...then she might have written the note, which got her killed. On the other hand, it could be a random note that was completely unrelated to either murder...no, I shook my head. Like Byron said, coincidences *were* rare. More than likely, the note was related to the case, which meant the police should have it.

I let the book fall closed and balanced it on my knees as I contemplated what I should do. If it was a blackmail note what was it doing in Annie's book? Why would Annie have it? Had she picked it up randomly and used it as a bookmark without noticing what was written on it? Unlikely.

I shifted a little in the bed and the book wobbled, but didn't fall. I didn't like the train of thought that my mind was running on, but it had to be considered. Annie had found Mia. She had been the first one on the scene and alone for a little while—a minute at least, maybe longer, from the time she left our table in the dining room until we heard her scream. It wouldn't take a long time to cut someone's throat. And she did have blood on her. Not a lot, that was true. Perhaps she'd used a glove out of the lost and found—Elise's glove—but hadn't been able to completely avoid getting blood on herself. She could have hidden the glove somehow...in a plastic bag maybe...to dispose of later, and she smeared some blood on the light switch to give her an excuse for her bloody hand.

My heartbeat kicked up as another thought hit me. Perhaps she gave the glove to Dominic to get rid of. He was supposedly out of the hotel when Mia died, but we didn't know exactly when he left. He could have stuffed it down the grate into the drain on his way to a shop. If she had wrapped it in something else...a bag or another cloth, then he could avoid getting blood on his hands and could return with his shopping bag of light bulbs and an alibi.

I rubbed a hand over my face and sighed. It was all very iffy and speculative. And why would you keep a blackmail note? Wouldn't you destroy it immediately?

I shifted to another point. If the note was intended for Annie—if Mia had seen or knew somehow that Annie had killed Cyrus—then why had Annie killed Cyrus? They were old friends and on good terms as far as I could see. In fact, Annie was about the *only* person Cyrus had seemed to get along with, and Annie seemed to be the only person to grieve for him. Was it guilt, not grief, that she struggled with?

I reached for my phone and typed out a text to Alex. *Are you awake?* I wanted to show him the note and talk it over with him. He was a good sounding board and much better at reading people—had I been completely wrong about Annie?— and I wanted to hear what he had to say.

But after several minutes ticked by, I decided he must have silenced the ringer on his phone or turned it off. I contemplated using the hotels' phone or creeping down the stairs and tapping on his door, but decided against it.

I could be totally wrong about the note and my assumptions about Annie. She might be innocent and the note had been planted there by the real murderer to throw suspicion on her. But that seemed an odd way to go about bringing a suspect to the attention of the police. They'd have to find that note in her book, and how could they do that if the book was stuffed down between the side of the chair and the cushion? My thoughts were bouncing and bumping around in my head like a bee trapped in a jar.

I was more confused now than I had been before I found the note. In any case, whether the note meant Annie was part of the suspect pool or not, Felix was definitely a suspect because of his lack of alibis. I hated even thinking that he could be remotely involved, but it wouldn't be smart to wake Alex to show him the note because the commotion would probably wake Felix as well. No, the best thing to do would be to contact the police first thing in the morning and turn it over to them. I could tell Alex about it in the morning, too. It would be easier to be alone with Alex tomorrow without drawing attention to ourselves.

I put the book back in my makeup bag and snuggled down under the covers, but I couldn't drift into sleep. I noticed the faint pulse of music from the bar down the street, something that I hadn't even been aware of when I was engrossed in thinking about the note, but now that I was trying to fall asleep, I could hear it distinctly.

After fifteen minutes, I threw the covers back and dug out the book again. I snapped a picture of the note with my phone, then crept over to feel through the pockets of my coat for Byron's business card. Yes, it was still there. I sent him a short text, saying that I'd found the note in a book at the hotel and thought he would want to know about it. I attached the picture, hid the book again, and got back into bed, which was now chilly.

I curled into a ball and tried to clear my mind, but the sheets weren't even warm before my phone rang. I snatched it off the little nightstand between the two beds, nearly yanking the charging cord from the wall. Melissa snorted and rolled over.

"Ms. Sharp, this is DCI Byron here. I received your text. I'm sending someone over to pick up the item immediately."

"Um—okay," I said. "I'll go downstairs and watch. Will it be someone in uniform?"

"No, it will be DS Gadd."

"All right." I gave Byron the night latch code because I wasn't sure if the hotel had an alarm system that activated after a certain time of night. If it did, using the code would keep it from sounding and waking everyone. "He can open the door with that code," I said. "I'll wait in the parlor for him."

I got out of bed again, thinking that at this rate it would be dawn before I actually got to sleep at all, but when I checked the time it was only a little after two. I slipped an oversized sweater over my flannel pajamas and tugged on a pair of thick socks, then I grabbed my phone. The battery was low, but it should last long enough to serve as a flashlight to let me navigate through the parlor without knocking a shin against any furniture.

CHAPTER 21

WITHIN A FEW MINUTES, I was sitting in the dim parlor in the same club chair by the bow window, my feet curled up under me. Instead of turning on lights as I moved, I'd used the light of my phone. I didn't know where the light switches were and figured I'd turn on a lamp, but once I sat down, I decided I didn't want to wake Annie or Dominic by turning on any lights. I wanted to avoid having to answer any awkward questions about why a police officer was coming by the hotel in the middle of the night.

As the display of my phone faded to black, darkness returned to the room, except for the square patch of light from the street lamp that glowed outside the window. The panes of the window cut the illuminated square into a grid of light and shadow that fell over my chair.

Down the street, one of the bars was still open, and I watched a couple leave, arm in arm. Their voices and footsteps echoed along the quiet street as they passed the window. After they disappeared around the corner, it was quiet except for the throb of music from the bar, which was louder now that I was on street-level and near a window.

On the opposite end of the street from the bar, I could see the soaring towers of the Abbey, which were now dark. Even though the floodlights were off, I could see the tower and its pinnacles, a black silhouette against the night sky. Near the Abbey, but a little closer to the hotel, the high wall with its balustrade enclosed the bulk of the Roman Baths. I couldn't see any drifts of vapor, but I knew steam was rising from the Great Bath, curling up into the cold air behind the wall. A hot bath sounded lovely. I wished I'd slipped on some shoes. My toes were freezing despite my thick socks.

I figured it would take Gadd a while to get to the hotel, so I settled in to wait. The hotel was quiet except for the low hum from one of the kitchen appliances and the faint hiss of the radiator. I checked my email on my phone and opened some of the other apps, but I couldn't concentrate. I heard a faint creaking sound and listened, thinking that someone had opened a door upstairs, but I didn't hear anything else, no tread on the stairs or squeak of a floorboard. I decided it must have been the building settling. I was fidgety so I occupied myself with trying to identify the songs I could faintly hear that were being played down the street at the bar. After fifteen minutes went by, I began to wonder if I should contact Byron, but then I told myself I was being impatient.

I picked up a brochure for the hotel that was lying on the end table and angled it so that the light from the street lamp illuminated it as I skimmed it. On the back page, a box highlighted the history of the hotel, touching on the building's different uses, mentioning the tannery and the casino. I read the next line then stopped and reread it.

"The hotel was once connected to the underground tunnels, or catacombs, of Bath. When the hotel was divided into individual residences each occupant had an entrance to the tunnels. Most of these entrances have been sealed, but the hotel still uses a small area of the tunnels for storage."

"Catacombs," I murmured to myself, looking out the window for a second. I scanned the rest of the text on the brochure, but it didn't say how extensive the catacombs were. Did the tunnels under the hotel stretch all the way to the Baths? I knew the Baths themselves had tunnels because they ran tunnel tours. I'd seen the brochure for those tours the day I toured the Roman Baths. If the tunnels under the Baths stretched to the hotel, then everything we'd thought about Cyrus's death could be wrong. What if he'd never left the hotel?

Since Cyrus was found in the Baths, everyone had assumed he'd died after they opened at nine thirty, but what if that wasn't what happened? I tapped the brochure against the edge of the chair, thinking of what Mia had said when I first asked her about Cyrus. She'd said she'd brought him another cup of tea and that he'd left after, during the rush. What if she hadn't actually *seen* Cyrus leave, only seen his empty place and assumed he'd left the hotel? If she was busy with other customers she probably hadn't been watching him every moment.

He might have left the dining room and been detoured downstairs where he was killed. It was quiet and secluded in the basement area. And then the killer would only have to transport his body to the Baths and leave it there to be discovered.

If Mia worked out what happened and threatened to expose the murderer…I shivered and it had nothing to do with my cold feet. Mia had been curious about Cyrus's death that morning in the Pump Room. I could picture her asking questions and poking around until she found out more. She also worked at the hotel, so she probably knew about the tunnels in the hotel, and since she worked at the Pump Room as well, I bet she knew about the tunnels at the Baths, too.

I shifted in the chair, and looked up and down the street again. Where was Constable Gadd? If Cyrus had been killed in the hotel and moved to the Baths, then it let Annie out. She could barely get down the stairs. I didn't think she could transport a body through a catacomb tunnel and get him into the Baths, especially someone as tall and heavy as Cyrus.

I doubted Elise knew about the tunnels, so she was probably out of the running as well. And it was questionable that Felix knew either. He knew Annie and Dominic from years ago, but he apparently hadn't kept up with them or ever stayed in the Bath Spa Hotel before.

A movement on the street caught my eye, and I strained to see better, but it was only another person leaving the bar. I picked up my phone to call Byron, but heard the unmistakable ring of a foot on the metal steps of the basement's iron staircase.

No one should be downstairs in the basement now. Everyone was in bed.

Nevertheless, someone was trotting up the stairs. Without thinking about why I was doing it, I clicked my phone so that the screen went dark. I tensed and was about to either dart across the room to the stairs or to the entry where I wouldn't be in the person's line of sight when they emerged into the parlor. But the second I spent hesitating meant that it was too late.

The back of a head became visible, then shoulders, as the person strode briskly up the stairs. Their quick pace brought them up the last twist of the stairs, and Dominic emerged into the parlor.

The room was dim, but the glow from the street lamp gave off enough light that I could see he was fully dressed in jeans and a dark sweater. From the knees down, his jeans were covered in a fine dirt, and he was brushing at them and the arms of his sweater as he walked.

Of course it wasn't Annie who was the murderer. It was Dominic. My heartbeat kicked into a skittery rhythm at the thought. He was big enough to carry Cyrus's body through the tunnels. Hadn't Dominic said something about Annie volunteering at the Baths and leading tours? She'd know about the tunnel tours. He could have found out about the tunnels from her, if he hadn't explored them himself. They were connected to his office. And we only had Dominic's word that he was at the shop when Mia died. He could have killed her then slipped out and stuffed the glove down the grate, then sprinted to the shop to establish an alibi.

I held my breath, thinking I should look away, but couldn't. Unmoving, like a rat mesmerized by the sway of a cobra, I watched him, amazed at his relaxed stride. He wasn't worried or jumpy. He was almost at the threshold of the kitchen. Another second, and he'd be gone.

He gave his sleeve another final brush and shifted his head slightly to check his elbow. Our gazes connected, and his steps faltered.

"Kate? Is that you?" He closed the distance before I even had time to stand.

"Yes. I couldn't sleep." My heartbeat hammered, and I felt breathless. Could he tell from my voice?

"So you came down here to sit in the dark?" he said, his voice filled with laughter. "You know, I see a lot of strange things in this business, but I have to admit that this is a first."

"I thought a change of scene might help."

"Well...okay." He hesitated as if he wasn't sure what to say, then his gaze focused on my lap.

I glanced down. The streetlight's glow picked out the blank screen of my phone, which was resting on top of the copy of *Northanger Abbey*.

His face changed, the jovial expression shifting into something guarded and wary.

I worked my feet out from under me. "I was just going back upstairs—"

He lunged suddenly, his arm lifted. I dodged, but my head snapped down as white spots exploded in my vision. For a few seconds, I had a fuzzy impression of him closing in, then his dirty sweater engulfed me, and there was only blackness.

CHAPTER 22

THE SMELL OF DIRT FILLED my nostrils, and everything was dark.

I thought for a second that my face was still pressed into Dominic's dusty sweater. I recoiled, but a pain shot through my head, and my stomach heaved. I stilled and waited for my insides to calm down.

I breathed in and out unsteadily. I realized it wasn't Dominic's sweater that was creating the blackness. It was darkness…all around me. My cheek was pressed to a hard, cold surface. My head throbbed with the worst headache I'd ever had. It felt as if someone were inside my skull banging away like a carpenter framing a house.

After a little bit, I brushed my hands around and traced a few oblong rectangles. Flagstones. A flagstone floor. My fingertips were gritty now from the layer of fine dust that covered the stones.

Cautiously, I sat up, and a feeling of lightheadedness swept over me, but it faded after a few seconds. The drumbeat in my head was still there, but it was minor compared to the fear rising inside of me. I ran my fingertips gently over my skull and found a tender goose-egg swelling behind my ear. I thought of Cyrus. I'd been much luckier than him. That thought galvanized me, and although the pain was still there, it didn't matter as much. For some reason, Dominic hadn't killed me—yet.

I patted my pockets, looking for my phone, then remembered I was in my flannel pajamas, which didn't have pockets. My phone wasn't on me. Of course, Dominic wouldn't be so stupid as to leave my cell phone with me. I patted the floor in ever widening circles just to make sure, but I only found more grit.

I shifted around and saw a thread of light across the floor behind me. I got to my feet, again feeling a flash of nausea as I shifted positions, but it cleared. The throb in my head continued, but didn't crescendo, so I kept my gaze fixed on the streak of light. I made my way slowly through the darkness, waving my arms in front of me like a creature in a zombie movie.

When the line of light illuminated my dirty socks, my fingers connected with a surface of shallow lines running through it—wood, I realized. I patted and found the edge, letting my fingers trail over the arch above my head and down the side until I found a cold metal handle. It was the arched doorway inside Dominic's office that led to the storage area. Unfortunately, I was on the other side of the door from Dominic's office, locked in the storage area.

I tugged and pulled on the handle, but the door was solid and didn't budge an inch. I remembered with a sinking feeling the secure latch I'd seen on the other side of the door when I came down to the office to pick up the papers for Annie.

I pounded on the door a few times with my fist and gathered my breath, then screamed for help, but broke off before I'd gotten more than a breathy syllable out. The effort had caused the single bass note that had been drumming in my head to burst into a full symphony of clanging pain. I thought I would pass out for a moment and rested my head against the cool grain of the wood until the worst of it passed. Then I pushed away from the door. Wherever Dominic was, I didn't want to summon him back. My screams in the basement wouldn't be heard several floors above...unless there was some sort of venting or ductwork down here.

The brochure said this area was used as a storeroom. That meant there had to be a light here somewhere. I traced my fingers along the edge of the wall on the side of the door near the handle, but didn't find a switch. I turned and made my way, again zombie-like, across the flagstones, but this time I waved my arms higher. I stumbled into something cold and chest-high.

I ran my hands over the smooth squared-off metal and encountered several handles spaced down the front—a filing cabinet. It wasn't locked, and I rifled through the drawers, but only felt paper. I resumed my slow progress, waving my arms in the air. After a few more steps, my fingers brushed against a string. I tugged, and a single light bulb came on.

Pain stabbed through my head at the sudden brightness. It took a few seconds for my eyes to adjust, but when they did, I realized the bulb was actually rather dim. It threw a weak circle of light around the room, illuminating a square room with a few more filing cabinets, a set of shelves, and several stacks of cardboard file boxes, but no convenient plumbing lines or vents.

I went back to the door, pulled and pushed and checked the hinges. There was no way I'd be able to get out this way. It was a solid piece of workmanship, built long ago before plastic and pressboard even existed.

I turned away—slowly to keep the nausea at bay—and looked around the room again. That's when I noticed another arched doorframe on the far side of the room. It was almost completely hidden by a stack of boxes, but it was obvious from the marks in the dirt that they'd been moved recently. Someone had shifted them forward enough to get the door open. And the best part was that the door didn't have a lock on it, only a single pin dropped down through a latch to keep the door closed.

I removed the pin and dragged the door open. It scraped across the flagstones with a creak, and a chilly breeze swept over me. That creak I'd heard earlier hadn't been the building settling. It must have been this door to the tunnels groaning on its hinges.

I'd forgotten for a little bit how cold I was, but the draft of air reminded me. The storeroom wasn't warm, but it was several degrees warmer than the tunnel in front of me. Flannel pajamas are definitely not the best attire for exploring catacombs, but I certainly wasn't going to wait around the storage room. As I went through the door, my gaze caught on the set of shelves positioned next to the door, which contained mostly file boxes, but a heavy flashlight with several dusty fingerprints visible on the barrel also stood on the edge of one shelf.

I snatched it up and pulled the door closed. It rasped over the flagstones as I switched on the light. I never would have thought that I'd be glad to make my way through catacombs in the middle of the night alone, but it was a definite improvement over being locked in the storage room.

I ran the beam of the flashlight around. I was in a tunnel with rough rock walls and ceiling, which was low enough that I had to duck my head as I walked forward, but not so low that it felt claustrophobic. I could hear the *plink* of water as it dripped slowly, but this area of the tunnel was dry. The thought of Dominic returning propelled me forward, but I didn't want to get lost in the tunnels either. Unfortunately, I didn't have any string or breadcrumbs on me, but as I moved forward in my little circle of light, I noticed a footprint in the dirt. When I placed my socked foot inside it, my foot almost looked petite, so a man's shoe. It was flat soled and had left a grid print. I bet it was from Dominic's shoe. From the lack of lights and other footprints, the tunnel certainly didn't look like it was used frequently.

I moved forward, and the walls narrowed, which made me nervous, but then the passageway widened. I came to a junction where the flashlight picked out several other tunnels branching away from it. I stood uncertainly for a moment, then shifted the flashlight to the ground. Someone in large shoes with a grid pattern on flat soles had walked across the open area to the tunnel that branched to the left. The footprints weren't in a neat unbroken line, but there were enough of them that I could see someone had walked that direction, then returned.

I crossed the open space and entered the other tunnel following the footprints. After a few yards, I had to slow down to pick my way through debris. Rocks, chunks of what looked like marble and other stones, littered the ground along with sections of pipes tinted orange with rust that looked like the Roman pipes that I had seen in the museum. The sound of water dripping became more frequent. Overhead, tiny stalactites only a few inches long hung down from the ceiling. The passageway turned, and the walls changed from rock to stones set in masonry.

I came to a stone archway, and the passage widened even more. I was glad to see that the walls became smooth with wires and modern pipes snaking along them, but debris still covered the ground.

Ahead, the flashlight's glow picked out a metal gate. Heart thumping, I scrambled over the last few rocks, expecting to see a padlock holding the door closed. I did not want to have to retrace my steps and risk running into Dominic.

When I reached the gate, I found it was closed, but not locked. The metal latch had been neatly sliced so that the gate swung free at my touch. Someone—it must have been Dominic—had used a bolt cutter or some similar tool to slice through the metal lock. The gate swung back with only a faint squeak.

A whisper of noise made me glance back over my shoulder and swivel the flashlight behind me. But it was only a loose section of wire that I must have disturbed. The end of it slithered off a piece of stone to the ground, and I let out a slow breath.

I felt flushed with the heat of an adrenaline rush and chilled to the bone at the same time. My heart pounded, but the coldness from the stones seeped through my now slightly damp socks, and the layers of my sweater and pajamas didn't do much to insulate me from the chilly air of the passageway.

Shivering, I tucked my elbows into my sides to conserve a little body heat and moved on. This section of the tunnel was even wider and higher and had more decorative arches and stairs. I heard a noise that sounded like laughter and stopped in my tracks.

Yes, there it was again. I took a few cautious steps forward, and saw a pattern of stripes—shadows—falling on the rough floor of the passageway. I tilted the flashlight up as I hurried forward. A metal grill was set in the ceiling.

The laughter rang out again, a higher pitched tone than Dominic's deep voice. I zigzagged the light across the grill and shouted, "Hello!"

The light caught the outline of shoes as someone walked over the grill. "Hey! Can you hear me?" I called.

I could hear a male voice suffused with laughter. "Mate, I've had one too many. I'm hearing voices."

"No, wait." I waved the flashlight frantically. "Down here. Look down. I'm under the grill."

A face appeared where the feet had been. I couldn't see much, only a faint pale circle of a young man's face and a swath of hair that fell forward as he bent to peer through the iron bars. I shifted the angle of the flashlight so that it illuminated more of me than the grill. "Thank goodness. Please, call the police. Ask for DCI Byron—"

"There's a girl down here," he called to someone behind him, and a shout answered him. "No, I'm not sloshed. Well, yes, I am, I suppose. But I know what I'm looking at. It's a girl under the grill." This seemed to strike him as incredibly funny, and he tumbled sideways as giggles overcame him while he repeated the phrase.

"This is incredibly important," I said, my voice shaking. "You've got to pull yourself together and call—"

The guy's friend reached him. "Up you come. You're hallucinating."

"No, he's not," I said, and waved the flashlight over the grill again. I gripped the wall below the grill, found a toehold on the cold rock wall, and pulled myself up a few feet. "I'm down here." But the giggling kid had rolled over the grill.

Then a deep, commanding voice shouted something that stripped the laughter out of both of them. The second guy caught the first guy's collar and hauled him to his feet as he said, "Come on. We've got to shove on."

I dropped back down to the ground and clicked the flashlight off. What if it were Dominic out there on the street?

I shifted to the darkness away from the moonlight. But wouldn't it be more likely Dominic was in the hotel? If he was in the hotel, why had he gone off and left me in the storage room? Maybe he was out walking the streets of Bath on some errand. I didn't want to think about what kind of errand he might be running after leaving me unconscious in the basement in the middle of the night.

If it wasn't Dominic, it might be a sober person I could flag down and ask for help. I might not have another chance to catch someone's attention. The streets of Bath weren't packed in the middle of the night like they were during the day.

I gripped the barrel of the flashlight, ready to click it on in an instant if I could distinguish that the person wasn't Dominic.

A figure appeared, crouching low next to the grill. Again, the slats of the grill made it hard to see the person, but I could distinguish pale blond hair, not dark hair like Dominic had. I surged forward, clicking on the flashlight. "Wait! Don't go. I need help."

"Ms. Sharp, is that you?"

"Constable Gadd," I said, as a surge of relief washed through me.

"Yes, ma'am. What's happened? I went to the hotel, but Mr. Bell said you'd gone back to bed and told him to tell me that it was all a mistake."

I groaned. "Of course," I said. "He left me in the basement to deal with you. He must have read the texts on my phone and knew you were on the way."

"I'm afraid, I'm not following you."

"He killed Cyrus and Mia."

"Dominic Bell?"

"Yes. I found out that the hotel is connected to the catacombs, and I found a note in a book, Annie's book, and worked it out. Mia must have threatened to blackmail him. She must have realized that Cyrus never left the hotel the morning he died."

I wondered if he thought I was a crazy woman, talking

to him from underground, but I pressed on, hoping that he would at least understand how dangerous Dominic was. "I think Cyrus was killed and taken to the Baths through these tunnels. Dominic is the only person with the knowledge and the strength to move Cyrus's body. Mia must have threatened him, so he killed her, too. Then he planted the blackmail note in Annie's book to throw suspicion on her—at least that's what I think happened, and it must not be too far off. He hit me and knocked me out when he realized I'd worked it out. I woke up in the hotel's storage room in the basement. He'd locked me in, but I found the door to these tunnels and got out that way."

"But Ms. DuPont's gloves..."

"She lost them, exactly as she said. Dominic must have taken the first glove he touched in the lost and found and put it on before he killed Mia. It happened to be Elise's glove."

Gadd rocked back on his heels. "I've heard about the catacombs, but never thought..."

"Look, you need to do something quickly. Since Dominic got rid of you, he'll go back to the storage room, and when he finds I'm not there—"

I heard a faint screeching noise, echoing along the stone passageways, and knew instantly that it was the door from the storage room to the tunnel being dragged across the flagstones as it was pulled open.

I clicked off the flashlight. Gadd must have heard it, too, because he lowered his voice. "He didn't get rid of me. I've already called DCI Byron." As he spoke, he pulled and tested the grill. "I was loitering about, waiting for DCI

Byron to arrive before going back to the hotel. That's when I saw those two youths and told them to move along."

He sat back on his heels. "It's no use. The grill is fixed good and tight. Can't get it up without tools. You find a quiet corner to hide in—should be plenty of nooks and crannies down there—DCI Byron and I will be along in a moment."

I nodded, not wanting to speak. The sound of the scrape had been much louder than Gadd's whispers, but I didn't want to risk making any noise at all. I had pulled myself up as high as I could to get closer to the grill to speak to Gadd, so now I carefully lowered myself to the ground.

I glanced down the tunnel in the direction that I'd come from. Still dark. I took a few steps away from the grill. After I cleared the moonlit patch of ground, I risked turning on the flashlight for a moment then made my way up a short set of stairs, still moving in the opposite direction from the storage room. I went through another gate that was propped open. Here, the passageway bent, and before I slipped around the corner, I glanced back.

A brief flash of light illuminated some stones at the end of the tunnel.

I shot forward along the dark passage, figuring I only had a few moments before Dominic caught up with me. Before I flicked off the flashlight, I had a quick glimpse of what looked like iron support beams that crossed the ceiling overhead. I turned off the light and felt my way into a large open room. I risked another sweep of the light around quickly. It was a good thing that I did.

Several more modern-looking bricked columns

marched across the center of the room, reaching up from square brick bases, which were set in what had once been a rectangular pool, to the ceiling above. The flashlight beam glanced on the few feet of murky water at the bottom of the pool and briefly illuminated the mossy walls that dropped several feet down to the water. A few steps in the wrong direction in the dark, and I would have taken a nosedive into essentially an empty swimming pool. A ledge ran around the exterior of the pool, and I moved quickly around the edge, tucked myself up behind one of the square pillars that was on ground level, and doused the flashlight.

I fought to get my breathing under control, thinking *I knew the tunnels had to connect to the Baths.* Of course, this was the last way I wanted to find out for sure that my hunch was right—running around in the dark cold passages with Dominic looking for me. My back was to the area where I'd come in, but I was completely turned around and had no idea which part of the bath complex I was in. For all I knew, Dominic might circle around and enter the room some other way. I tensed at the tread of feet, and reminded myself to duck to the right, if he appeared in front of me, not left. To the left of me was the sharp drop to the pool.

A flashlight beam swept the room, flickering over the columns. It was behind me, thank goodness, and when it came to me, it threw a solid rectangular shadow of the pillar I was huddled against on the wall opposite. A drop of water plopped onto my head, and I started, but managed to not make an audible noise or move so much that I gave myself away.

He only paused for a second, then the footsteps resumed and faded. I gripped the flashlight with sweaty palms. Should I dart back along the tunnel the way I'd come? Could I make it back to the storage room before Dominic did? I doubted the door to the storage room was locked, but what if he knew a shortcut through the tunnels that would bring him back to the storage room more quickly than the route I would take?

I squeezed the flashlight with my slick palms. Wouldn't movement be better than sitting here in the dark? It could be hours before Byron arrived at the hotel, got inside, and made his way through all the tunnels.

I didn't like either option, but as much as I wanted out of the damp darkness, staying put seemed to be the better choice, and I settled in for a wait.

I don't know how long I sat there, but it *felt* like forever. When my legs began to get pins and needles, I decided I had to move a little. I hadn't heard anything for ages except the irregular plinks of water drops.

Using the pillar, I stood slowly, flexing my feet back and forth. A light hit me. It felt like a physical blow after the complete darkness.

"Ah, there you are."

CHAPTER 23

DOMINIC'S DEEP VOICE SOUNDED JUST the same—affable, good-natured, almost jokey. "I was beginning to think you'd never come out of your hiding spot. So glad you've shown yourself. Saves me from hunting among all the rocks for you before I toss you into the pool. Such an idiotic tourist thing to do, sneak about the Baths after hours. Such a shame you took a header into a deep empty pool," he said, his tone full of false regret. "Hiding was clever, I'll grant you that, but you left a nice trail of dusty footprints, and when I realized they'd petered out, I simply retraced my steps until I isolated where you must have turned off."

The thought flashed through my mind that it was ironic that I'd followed his footprints through the tunnels to the Baths, and then he'd followed my footprints to find me in the Baths. I had thrown up an arm to block the light, but I couldn't see him. I was on the short side of the rectangular pool, and it sounded from his voice as if he was on the longer side. "It's no good, Dominic," I said squinting into the light. "The police know what you did. They're on the way."

"Of course, you'd say that," he said then switched to a falsetto voice, "Don't kill me—all is known," He kept the light focused on my face, but I could tell from his voice that he was getting nearer, walking down the long edge of the pool.

I inched away from him, backing up from the pool's rim.

"Don't move," he said, his voice returning to its normal timbre. "I'd hate to have to shoot you first."

I swallowed. Did he have a gun? "That would rather blow the accidental death scenario you have planned," I said, with my feet planted.

"Yes, it would. I much prefer the storyline that you were so fascinated with catacombs that you explored them on your own and, stupidly, fell to your death, but I can work with anything. I prefer the quick bash on the head method. It worked so well with Cyrus. I couldn't believe my luck when he followed me downstairs to complain about his room. It came to me in an instant. The cobblestone paperweight was right there and exactly the right size to fit in the palm of my hand—rather good, that bit, I think—I'm glad I get to share it with someone. I brought it down good and hard and that was it. Much better than using the knife. I won't do that again. Too messy. But in the end, it doesn't matter to me how you die. I can work with anything. I'm light on my feet, as they say. Besides, I won't be around when they find you, so it hardly matters."

"I must disagree with you."

The voice came out of the darkness, and I turned toward it even though I couldn't see anything.

"I think you'll be around a long while," the voice continued. "But it will be in prison, of course."

Dominic whipped the flashlight in the direction I'd arrived from, illuminating Byron, who held a gun trained on him. Two police officers stood behind Byron.

Suddenly, several spots of light appeared, all of them focused on Dominic.

I saw that Dominic didn't have a gun. But gun or not, I dived back behind the pillar, and watched as Dominic turned to run away. In the growing light, I saw a flash of blond hair, and realized Gadd was positioned behind Dominic. He was pinned down with officers blocking his path both in front and behind him. The deep pool hemmed him in on the other side.

"I think you'd better come with us, Mr. Bell," Byron said. "I'd hate for things to get out of hand."

Dominic glanced back at Byron then raised his arms. "Fine. Fine. I know when I'm beaten." He turned and took a few steps toward Byron, then spun around and headed for Gadd, who was in position behind him, but Dominic's foot must have hit one of the gaps between the uneven flagstones. He tripped and fell, landing with his shoulder on the edge of the pool, his head over the edge. He flailed there a moment, his broad shoulders tilting toward the depths of the pool, then he went over the edge into the darkness.

I heard water spatter, and then Byron's sharp voice

calling for light. Byron and the rest of the officers rushed forward then halted at the rim of the pool. After a pause, he said, "Nothing we can do now, except see to Ms. Sharp." Most of the flashlights swung away from the pool to me.

I stepped out from behind the pillar as a voice said, "I'll see to her," and I didn't need a flashlight to know it was Alex. Someone helpfully trained a flashlight on him, and I closed the distance between us, going into the circle of his arms.

~

EVEN THOUGH IT was three o'clock in the morning every light was on at the hotel. Alex and I could see the glowing blocks of light shining out from the hotel's front windows from the end of the street where the car stopped, edging right up to the waist-high iron pylons that blocked off the street to vehicles.

"Here you are," said the constable who Byron had assigned to drive us back to the hotel. It was only a few blocks, but I was glad to accept the ride and avoid going back to the hotel through the darkness of the tunnels.

Byron had said a few sharp words to Alex that I missed, mostly because I had my head buried in Alex's shoulder. I had been in a daze, shaken at what I'd just seen—well, heard, to be specific. I'd kept my face turned away from the pool as Byron escorted us through the Baths to the main entrance, which was now unlocked. An officer had been stationed at the door, but at a nod from Byron, he'd let us pass and called for someone to take us to the hotel.

"The DCI should be along shortly," the constable added

as we climbed out of the car. He made a u-turn, heading back for the Baths. Lights blazed there, too. We could see them from the street, and hear the shout of voices behind the tall stone wall as the police investigated.

"How are you doing?" Alex asked. It was our first moment alone.

I shook my head. "Amazed to think that a little while ago I was creeping around there in the dark, hiding from Dominic." I shivered, and he wrapped an arm around me.

"Let's get you back to the hotel where you can warm up."

I looked up at him as we walked. "Byron didn't sound happy with you. How did you get into the Baths? And why are you even awake?"

"Something woke me—I'm not sure what, but I heard several male voices then heavy footfalls tromping through the hotel. I went to see what was happening. Byron was in the hotel with several other officers. He said they'd let themselves in with the night latch code you'd given Gadd. Then Byron told me the highlights of the chat you'd had with Gadd from the catacombs. Byron was coordinating with several other officers, who were on their way to enter the Baths through the main entrance. He was going in through the tunnels and the other men were to go in through the Bath's main entrance so they could trap Dominic. Byron ordered me to stay put in the hotel until you and Dominic were located."

"But you didn't stay put."

"I gave Byron and his entourage a head start, then followed them through the tunnels."

"Oh, Alex—"

"I wasn't about to sit quietly, knowing you were down in the tunnels, and Dominic was somewhere down there as well."

"You don't have to defend yourself to me. I'm so glad you were there. I'll admit, I was glad to see Byron, but seeing you—" I cleared my throat, and went on, "well, I don't think I've ever been happier to see anyone in my life. I mean, I know that sounds like a huge exaggeration—"

Alex said, "I know exactly what you mean."

A rectangle of light fell over us as the hotel's door opened. Melissa stepped outside, her robe fluttering around her as she surged down the short flight of steps. "Kate! Are you okay? You look like you've been rolling around in dirt. And your hands—they're freezing." She threw a reproachful look at Alex, and dragged me inside.

I blinked in the bright light and let Melissa guide me to a seat beside the fireplace. "Felix, you can get this started, can't you?" Melissa asked.

As my eyes adjusted, and I sorted out the figures moving around the crowded room, I realized everyone in the hotel was awake. Felix was already kneeling on the hearth, stacking wood. Paul, in a sweatshirt and flannel pants, stood looking a little bereft with his hands empty and no pencil or tablet to juggle. Even Elise was back, still in the cocktail dress she'd worn to the preview party, striding purposely back and forth across the room, her phone pressed to her ear, barking out sentences about disgraceful treatment and uncalled for allegations. As Elise whipped around and made her way back across the room, I saw Annie leaning heavily on her crutch, standing to one side in the archway of the darkened bar, her face pale and strained. Her gaze caught on mine, and she raised her eyebrows as she asked, "Dominic?"

I hesitated, unsure what to say.

It must have been enough of an answer for her because her good knee buckled, and she sagged against the door-frame. The crutch hit the floor as she pressed the fingertips of both hands to her lips. Alex went to her and guided her into a nearby chair. She closed her eyes for a moment, then refocused on me. "Is he...?"

I shook my head. "I'm sorry."

Annie made a whimpering sound, which drew Elise's attention. She ended her call, noticed me in the chair, and raised her eyebrows in shock. "Will someone please tell me what is going on here?" Elise looked sharply at Paul, but he shrugged. Elise riveted her gaze back on me. "Well? I know *I* have a reason to be up at this time of the morning since the police just now seemed to get it through their heads that I've been telling them the truth—" I quirked an eyebrow at her, thinking of the underhanded method she'd used to get Cyrus's cell phone, and she added, "—about my *gloves*, but why is everyone else up?"

"It has to do with Cyrus and Mia," I said slowly, glancing at Annie. "Dominic..." I trailed off because Annie's face was so white, I wondered if she was going to faint, but she drew in a deep breath.

"I knew it," she said, her gaze focused on the floor. "He did it. He murdered them. He murdered them both."

A stunned silence fell over the room, except for the crackle of the fire, which Felix now had going. Annie let out a shaky breath and looked at me. "I had no proof. I suspected, but you worked it out, didn't you?"

"Not until tonight."

The sound of the hotel's door opening caused all of us to jump. Byron entered, glanced around the room, and said, "Well, perhaps it is better this way. With everyone up, I can get statements from you all. Mrs. Bell, may I speak to you alone for a moment?" Looking miserable, she nodded and gripped the side of the chair to lift herself out of it as if she weighed a great deal more than her petite frame possibly could. Paul rushed to hand her the crutch, and Annie slipped it under her arm then motioned for Byron to follow her to the back of the hotel to their private quarters.

As Byron left with another officer following him, he looked back over his shoulder at Gadd, who had slipped into the room. Byron nodded to an unoccupied chair by the window, the one I'd sat in a few hours earlier as I waited for Gadd to arrive to collect the note I'd found.

Gadd worked a pair of plastic gloves onto his hands, then ran them along the edge of the chair and removed something. "That's the book I found," I said, recognizing the cover as he examined it. "It was there in between the cushion and the side of the chair. It was put back...?"

Gadd flipped through the book and nodded with satisfaction as the note appeared between the pages. "Just where our anonymous tip said it would be."

" An anonymous tip...? Oh," I said, as the truth dawned on me. "Dominic put it back. *He* called in a tip, telling the police where to find the blackmail note, hoping that because it was in Annie's book it would implicate her."

Gadd said, "Yes, that's what we think. We traced the call. It was placed from a landline at a bar one block away. The fact that the book and note were replaced after Mr. Bell discovered you with them, indicates that he replaced them so we could find them in the place where the tipster said they would be. We would have checked out the tip immediately—it came in earlier tonight—but we had Ms. DuPont to question, and we often get a lot of tips in cases like this that draw a lot of media attention. I think the DCI wanted to finish with her first, but then we got your message, Ms. Sharp, about the note. We knew we had to get over here quickly." He pressed his lips together for a moment. "I came as fast as I could."

"I'm sure you did your best," I said. A crystal tumbler appeared before my nose.

"Drink this," Felix said. "You look like you need it." He had poured himself a drink as well and took a gulp without blinking. "I know I do."

My feet were warming up, and I wasn't shivering, but I took the tumbler and sipped. I sputtered as the drink burned down my throat.

"Will someone please explain to me exactly what has happened?" Elise demanded.

"I'll be happy to bring you up to speed," Byron said as he reentered the room alone. "Dominic Bell was in a relationship with Octavia Blakely. She contacted me late this evening, to tell me that she believed Dominic killed Cyrus."

I glanced at Felix. Unlike his usual posture of languid aloofness, he stood tensely, all his attention on Byron. "Why? Did he confess?"

"No. It was the news of Mia Warren's death here at the hotel that made Mrs. Blakely suspicious. She said Mr. Bell had occasionally joked about doing away with Mr. Blakely, but that once a few months ago, he had seriously tried to convince her to contrive some sort of fatal accident so that she would be a widow—a very wealthy widow. Prior to that, Mr. Bell had tried to convince her to divorce Mr. Blakely, but she refused because it would put her in some financial difficulty. She was quite forthright with me about her financial situation."

"She didn't want to be poor," Felix said. He tossed back the rest of his drink, then set the tumbler on the mantle. "At least she's honest about it. She probably gave Dominic the same speech she gave me years ago. She loved me, but she wouldn't marry me. She couldn't stand being poor, not when other…options were available. Of course, her definition of poor is rather unusual. If you only have one house, or only a rented flat, then you are impoverished."

Byron's eyebrows drew together in a frown. "You didn't mention that your relationship with her was that close. You proposed marriage, and she turned you down?"

"That's about it. I didn't mention it because I didn't think it was relevant. Happened years ago."

"But you spent time with her these last few days," Byron said.

"Watching me, were you?" His face flushed. "And me behaving like a lovesick youth. I thought Octavia and I might…well…never mind. I was wrong. Just goes to show that even a crusty old bloke like me can be daft when it comes to love. She was only passing time with me." He cleared his throat. "But in any case, she never would have left Cyrus, I can tell you that. They had a prenuptial agreement. I assume that if she divorced him, she wouldn't get anything—or not enough by her standards, which are extremely high. But if she were a widow…then things would be different."

"Oh, yes," Byron said. "Quite different. As Mr. Blakely's widow she will inherit a hefty sum. We looked into it."

"So at the party it was *Dominic* that Octavia was staring at when she looked so frightened," I said as I looked at Felix. "He was standing a little distance behind you, and I thought it was you she was scared of. When she heard about Mia, she was so unnerved."

"And I thought she was upset with me for keeping the news from her," Felix said with a shake of his head.

Elise's sharp voice cut across Felix's melancholy tone as she said to Byron, "So you kept me up half the night, when you knew his wife had a motive to kill him?"

Byron's face remained impassive. "A glove embroidered with your initials and traces of blood on it was found in the drain a short distance from this hotel. We had no physical evidence to tie Mrs. Bell to either death."

"But I told you, I lost those gloves. Someone else—Dominic it seems—picked one up and used it."

"Yes, but it was physical evidence, which must always be investigated."

"If it was in the drain, why wasn't it swept away with the water?" Alex asked.

"We were fortunate that it hasn't rained for the last few days. Mr. Bell also helpfully wrapped the glove in a plastic carrier bag before shoving it down the drain, probably so that he could carry it through the street unnoticed. It protected the glove for us quite nicely and kept it from being contaminated by any other materials." He turned away from Elise and looked at Gadd. "Speaking of physical evidence…was it there?"

"Yes, sir." Gadd, who had been waiting on the side of the room, stepped forward and handed Byron the Jane Austen book and note.

Byron pulled on gloves, then separated the note from the book, put both in different clear plastic evidence bags, and sealed them, making notes on the outside of the bags. Then he leaned close under the light to look at the ragged edge of the note where it had been torn. He took another plastic bag from the inner pocket of his jacket, which contained a piece of paper. He aligned the two notes, and even with them encased in plastic, you could see that the rough, angled tear across the bottom of one note matched the tear across the top of the other piece of paper. "I believe it is a match," he said, then looked around the room. "Did anyone here, see these pieces of paper? Except Ms. Sharp, of course."

Byron walked slowly around the room, holding the papers so that everyone could see them. He had already moved by Paul, when Paul suddenly straightened from his position leaning against the wall. "Wait. Let me look at it again." He bent his head over the plastic bags. "When I left the dining room after breakfast on—Friday, I guess it would have been—I bumped into Dominic as I turned toward the stairs. He was ripping a paper in half, and I jogged his arm. He dropped one of the pieces. I picked it up and handed it to him. I think it was this one." He tapped one of the plastic bags. "I didn't read it, but I do remember it had a couple of words in blue ink."

"Excellent. Thank you. That is helpful." Byron put the plastic bags away and began to give Gadd and the other officers instructions.

"Well, aren't you going to tell us what it means?" Elise demanded. "I think we have a right to know."

CHAPTER 24

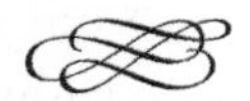

BYRON RAISED HIS EYEBROWS AT Elise's tone, but he said, "It is a blackmail note that Mia Warren wrote to Mr. Bell." He recited the words without taking the papers out of his pocket. "'You think no one knows, but I figured it out. I'll tell, if you don't pay.' I believe Mr. Bell must have been in the process of destroying the note when Mr. Alexander ran into him. Mr. Bell must have decided to keep both pieces of the note. We found half of the note on the floor of the office where Mia was killed. It must have fallen out of his pocket."

"That's why you wanted a sample of handwriting from each of us," I said, "to compare to the note."

Byron nodded. "At that point in the investigation, we weren't sure if the paper was a blackmail note or simply some other stray bit of paper. *You think no one knows, but I figured it out* does tend to cause one to think of blackmail but it could *possibly* have been something else, something unrelated to the crime. Having a sample of each person's handwriting allowed us to quickly determine it was probably Mia who had written the note. We are still waiting for the official analysis of the handwriting on the note, so gathering samples allowed us to move forward."

Alex said, "But getting back to Dominic. He still had part of the note?"

"Yes. He planted the fragment so that it would throw suspicion on someone else."

"Annie," I said with a shake of my head. "His wife. It was in her book."

"But it would have Mr. Alexander's fingerprints on it as well by now," Byron said, "as well as his own. But since it was written on a notepad from the hotel, his fingerprints would be expected...while Mr. Alexander's wouldn't be explained away so easily. Nice and confusing for us when we discovered it after his tip."

The sound of footsteps coming up the circular iron staircase from the basement drew everyone's attention. A young constable appeared, trotted up the remaining steps, and looked surprised to see so many people staring at him. He spotted Byron and went across the room to him, extending a man's leather shoe, which was encased in an evidence bag. "We found it, sir. Size twelve-point-five, silver buckle, and punch detailing on the toe."

"Good work," Byron replied. Peering through the plastic, he examined the interior of the shoe and gave a short nod. "Correct brand as well. Where was it?"

"In the smaller tunnel, the one with the debris."

I straightened in the chair. "That's why Dominic was in the tunnels in the middle of the night. He was looking for Cyrus's missing shoe."

Byron said, "Yes, it must have fallen off when he moved

the body from here to the Baths. If it were ever found and identified as Mr. Blakely's shoe it would show Blakely had been in the tunnels. And that was something that Mr. Bell did not want to risk. Originally, we believed that Mr. Blakely was killed after the Baths opened, at nine thirty. If this shoe was found, it would widen the time of death window. We already had a few questions about it, so a discovery of a personal item from the victim in a tunnel that connected the bath complex to the catacombs under the city itself…well, that would certainly have shifted the direction of the investigation."

"Questions about the time of death," I murmured. Now that I was warm and safe, my thoughts were spinning back over the last few days. "It was the rigor, wasn't it?"

Byron raised his eyebrows. "Yes. You are very observant. Why didn't you mention it before?"

"I didn't notice it—the doctor who examined Cyrus said something about the state of Cyrus's body. She thought that Cyrus had been dead several hours. But with everything else that happened that morning, I didn't think about what she'd said again until you mentioned it just now. And even the doctor said it was hard to judge time of death by rigor."

"It is rather tricky. The typical onset of rigor is generally between two to six hours after death, but a number of other factors, including the physical condition of the individual and the ambient temperature, cause variations. And then there are cases of cadaveric spasm, or instantaneous rigor, which is what the medical examiner suspects was the case with Mr. Blakely. The official report is not yet in, but with the statement Mr. Bell made to you combined with the evidence of the shoe in the tunnel, I believe we now have an accurate grasp of the events surrounding Mr. Bell's death, which of course, also answers the questions around Ms. Warren's death as well."

"Excellent," Elise said. "Now that all that bother has been settled, we can get back to work."

~

"DEPARTING AT TEN IN THE MORNING?" Felix asked three days later as he opened the door of the van and tossed in his tote bag. "You're going soft on us, Elise."

Alex and I were a few paces behind him with our suitcases and exchanged a glance. Felix had been unusually subdued for the last few days. Well, I supposed it wasn't that unusual for someone who'd been embarrassed in his romantic endeavors to go through a phase of withdrawal, but he'd let many opportunities for smart-alecky remarks slide by him.

Elise smiled at him with what I thought seemed to be an almost fond look. "Glad to see you're getting back to your typical snarky ways. I find that I've actually missed your snide comments these last few days."

"I don't know what you're talking about," Felix said rather gruffly.

Elise hadn't been joking when she said we could get back to work. She had soothed the backers and convinced them that the publicity over the deaths would only be a boost for the production. She also managed to get a new director on the team, someone she referred to as a "nice biddable man," which I supposed meant she felt she could manage him. He wasn't able to join us immediately, which only made Elise like him more.

Our team spent the last several days answering police questions, appearing at three inquests, and finishing our location scouting. Now that we'd been given the all-clear to leave from Byron and had all the scouting material we needed, we were wrapping up.

Elise looked over Felix's shoulder. "There's Annie, waving us down." Paul had parked the van at the end of the pedestrian walkway that ran in front of the street with the hotel. Annie was swinging her crutch quickly over the cobblestones. She looked as if she'd survived a bout with the flu with her face pale and thinner than it had been when we arrived. "Do go see what she needs, won't you Felix?" Elise asked.

I glanced at Elise curiously. Normally, she'd send Paul on an errand like that, but perhaps she had picked up on the easy camaraderie between Felix and Annie during the last couple of days.

Annie had been up and moving about the hotel the morning after learning the news about Dominic. She'd bustled about, fixing breakfast and attending to the details of running the hotel, waving anyone off who suggested that she take a break. Felix had been one of those people who tried to convince her to take it easy, but she'd said firmly and decisively, "No. I have to stay busy. It's the only thing I *can* do." But her voice had a ragged edge to it.

I'd been surprised when Felix nodded and said, "I can understand that." He'd taken a stack of dirty dishes from her, rolled up his sleeves, and washed them. We'd all pitched in to do what we could, but Felix had done more than anyone else. I'd even seen him vacuuming the carpet in the parlor this morning.

We had all tactfully avoided mentioning Octavia, and I think that Felix was grateful. She had been at Cyrus's inquest, but Felix had only nodded politely at her when their gazes crossed as we left the building. She'd barely acknowledged his presence with a faint dip of her head. I was walking beside him, and I think I was the only person who heard him mumble under his breath something about a lucky escape.

"I had to come out and say goodbye and apologize again for…well, everything," Annie said. Felix had met her halfway, but she'd waved him off and quickly covered the distance to the van.

"You don't have anything to apologize for," I said. "None of what happened was your fault."

Annie sighed. "Not directly, no. But perhaps if I'd spoken up when I began to suspect that Dominic was having an affair. If he knew that it wasn't a secret, then he might not have done what he did."

"Nonsense," Elise said in an unbending tone. "People like Dominic, once they've set their minds to something, they won't be deterred. No use ruining the rest of your life because someone else made terrible decisions. Now, what are your plans?"

Felix said, "Don't pry, Elise. It's too soon—"

Elise sent him a quelling look. "Annie's already decided, haven't you?"

Annie nodded. "Yes. I'm going to sell the hotel. I've made a few calls about it. It was more Dominic's dream than mine. I have an idea for a travel website, a bit of a gap in the market, so I'll see if that takes off. Then I want to travel, if it all works out. Soon I should have this thing off," she tapped her cast, "and then I'm off to see the world."

"Where will you go?" I asked.

"I'm not sure yet."

"Can't go wrong with the Lake District," Felix said, and then looked as if he wished he could take the words back. We were set to film in Bath after the New Year then return to the area around Nether Woodsmoor in the spring for the last episodes of the production. Nether Woodsmoor wasn't that far from the Lake District.

Annie sent him a quick grin. "I'll keep that in mind."

Elise looked at her watch. "We must get on the road. Are we loaded?" Elise asked, looking to Paul. "Paul!"

He looked up from his phone, and I wondered if he had been texting with Melissa. She had departed from Bath last night to return the extra clothing that had been used in the exhibit to its various lenders. I'd noticed Paul had offered to help load boxes for her, and when I asked how things were going before she left, Melissa had smiled dreamily. "We exchanged phone numbers, and he's already sent me a text," she said, which didn't sound all that romantic to me, but she seemed happy about it, so I was glad for her.

"Just two more suitcases." Paul looked at me and Alex.

We said goodbye to Annie, and went to the back of the van where Alex tossed in our suitcases.

"Well, not the trip we expected." I gazed one last time at the wall that enclosed the bath complex and the tower of the Abbey ranging up behind it.

"No, but at least the drive back should be less stressful."

"Alex!" a voice called, and I tried to hide a grimace. We

hadn't seen Viv in several days. Alex hadn't mentioned her, and I figured it was best to not raise the subject, superstitiously afraid that if I did utter her name, she might pop up instantly.

She jogged quickly toward us, her auburn hair bouncing around her like she was in a shampoo commercial. "Oh, don't say you're leaving."

"Afraid so," I said without a trace of sadness.

"Oh, that's too bad. I've been so busy at work the last few days, I couldn't get away, and I did so want to hear all about what happened. It's just too amazing."

"We have to get on the road," Alex said, looking toward Elise. "Boss's orders. It's been good to see—"

"That's your boss?" Viv asked, her eyes widening. "That's Elise DuPont, the producer?"

"Yes."

Viv took a deep breath and her manner changed from bouncy and outgoing to nervous. She licked her lips. "Do you think...could you...maybe give her my name?"

"Your name?" Alex asked.

"Yes, for when you film here in Bath. I'd do anything—be an extra or whatever—or if you're going to have auditions, I'd go where ever they are. Up to London or Manchester, or anywhere."

The tension that had appeared in Alex's shoulders the moment Viv called his name, disappeared. "You want a part. You want to be in the production."

"Yes," she said, looking uncomfortable. "I know it's a lot to ask, but if you could just mention my name to her, that could make a huge difference. I've taken acting classes, and I've been on *tons* of auditions. I even got a commercial. It was local, but that's something, right? Anyway, what I've found out is that, if you know someone it helps get your foot in the door. And when I heard what you were doing and that you'd be in Bath, I had to look you up. I mean, I'm glad to see you and catch up and everything, but..." her glance strayed to Elise again. "Anything you could do for me would be great."

Alex grinned. "Let me introduce you to Elise."

"Really?" Viv squeaked.

"Come on."

Viv tucked her hair behind her ears and smoothed down her windbreaker that she wore over running pants. "Do I look okay?" She asked, swiveling toward me.

She looked the complete opposite of a Regency miss, but I thought of all the ultra modern young women who showed up at the set on filming days dressed in ripped shorts and shirts that hung off their shoulders, but who later emerged from Costume swathed in high-waisted gowns, gloves, and bonnets. "You look great."

Elise was now in the driver's seat of the van, but the door was open. Alex approached Elise with Viv trailing along behind him. He made the introductions, Elise asked a few questions, then she sent Viv to talk to Paul. He gave her a business card. Viv turned away, squished up her shoulders and mouthed *thank you* to Alex before spinning and walking away, her stride so bouncy that I almost expected her to break into a skip.

"Well," Alex said. "That was...interesting. All that 'accidentally' running across our paths." He laughed. "She knew Elise's name and all about the production. She had researched everything."

"She was star-struck," I said. "She *didn't* want to be your girlfriend."

"I should find that a blow to my ego, but I'm actually relieved," Alex said. "She kept showing up and barging in."

"It was awkward," I agreed. As we moved around to climb in the van, I stopped. "Ah, Alex—she's coming back."

Viv was bouncing back toward us. She gripped Alex's arm. "I was so excited I completely forgot to tell you that I think you made exactly the right choice about the jewelry." She squeezed his arm, then turned to me and said in a fake whisper, "You'll love it. Okay, I am leaving now. Bye."

She gave a little wave and bounded off again.

Alex watched her retreating back for a moment then turned to me. "Just making sure she wasn't going to come back. She doesn't have the whole story." He pulled a small square box out of the pocket of his jacket.

I stared at the little box, my heart suddenly pounding.

The words *Alex, this is so sudden* were already forming in my mind when he flicked the hinged lid back. A pair of enormous gold chandelier earrings glinted against the black velvet background. The gold was fashioned in a mesh pattern and rows of spiky crystals lined the ragged bottom edge of the earrings. "Um—they're—ah…unusual."

"Unusually awful, I agree," Alex said. "They're for my mom."

"Oh," I said. "What a relief. I thought—"

"I know. It's what Viv thought, too. When she 'bumped' into me the other day, she followed me into the jewelry store. My mom has a bracelet like this, so I decided to get them. My mom is hard to buy for—people with appalling taste are, you know—so when I saw these, I thought they'd be perfect. Christmas is only a few weeks away."

"Right," I said, readjusting my thoughts. *Christmas gift for his mom. Not a ring.* I smiled as brightly as I could. "Good thing you saw them. I'm sure she'll…love them…?"

"Yeah…hard to imagine, but there you go. There's no accounting for taste." He snapped the box closed and dropped it in his pocket as he gestured for me to climb into the van ahead of him. "Now, I just have to find you a gift for Christmas."

I shifted around Felix to the seat behind him. "Christmas gifts," I said. "I hadn't even thought about them."

"Well, you better get on it," Elise said from the front seat. "You have to mail yours back to the States, right?"

"Yes, I suppose I better get busy." I said. Alex closed the door and came to sit beside me. Elise put the van in drive, and I twisted around for a last look at the tower of the Abbey, but my thoughts were a jumble.

Why had I thought it was a ring? Did I really think Alex was going to pop the question, standing on a street with our work colleagues looking on? I'd told him that I didn't want anything to change in our relationship. I liked things the way they were. Didn't I? Then why had I felt a flare of disappointment—just a tiny one—when I saw that they were earrings? I pushed that thought away.

Alex and Elise were right. Christmas wasn't that far away. But it wasn't the gifts that had to be mailed that I was suddenly concerned with. What in the world was I going to get Alex for Christmas? I had weeks to work it out. No need to stress about it now. Plenty of time…but somehow I thought I was going to need all of that time to find the perfect gift.

THE END

~

Stay up to date with with Sara. Sign up for her updates and get exclusive content and giveaways.

~

Don't miss Kate's next adventure, a Christmas novella, Menace at the Christmas Market. Available in ebook, audio, and print.

A Christmas novella in an English village

WITH THE HOLIDAYS NEARING, Kate has time off, a rare occurrence for a location scout. The Jane Austen documentary series is in a production lull, and she plans to spend her time searching for the perfect Christmas gift for Alex, which has turned out to be a task as difficult as finding an unspoiled location for a medieval-inspired fantasy series.

Kate goes to the local Regency-themed Christmas Market in search of a gift, but a new acquaintance is poisoned. Kate is drawn into the investigation and soon realizes she must discover who wants to make sure she doesn't ring in the New Year.

Menace at the Christmas Market is the fifth standalone installment in the Murder on Location cozy mystery series. Celebrate the holiday season with this fun Christmas novella from *USA Today* bestselling author Sara Rosett today!

THE STORY BEHIND THE STORY

Thanks for reading *Death in an Elegant City*. Kate and Alex will encounter another mystery soon. If you'd like to know when I have a new book out, you can sign up for my newsletter at SaraRosett.com/signup/2, which will get you exclusive excerpts of upcoming books and access member-only giveaways.

When I came up with the idea of writing a contemporary mystery series related to Jane Austen, I knew that Bath would be a potential setting for one of the books. I had read about Bath and wanted to visit it for years, but I couldn't write about it until I actually traveled there. Happily, I was able to go to Bath last year and experience it firsthand. You can see some of my travel photos as well as images of places that inspired me at my pinboard for the book on Pinterest.

I had an idea for *Death in an Elegant City*, a scouting trip that goes horribly wrong, but the pieces of the plot didn't gel until I was in Bath. I had read about Bath Abbey's clock tower and thought it would be a great location for the climax of the book. Climbing over the vaults of the Abbey behind the clock face sounded very Hitchcockesque. But when I toured the clock tower, I realized the idea wouldn't work. The tower was too restricted and I couldn't figure out how to get both Kate and the villain in the clock tower without resorting to breaking the rule of having Kate behave in a TSTL manner, which stands for Too Stupid To Live. (Protagonists says, "I know it's after midnight, I'm alone, and I feel as if someone is following me, but I'll go ahead and climb these stairs to the lonely clock tower and see what happens...") Fortunately, when I toured the Roman Baths I found a perfect setting for the finale of the book. It was suitably mysterious, and the location had a tie with Jane Austen. The hotel as well as the owners and employees in the book are entirely fictional, but one part of the book was inspired by the hotel I stayed in while in Bath. When I learned that it was once connected to the catacombs under Bath the main points of the plot fell into place. If you go to Bath, you can tour the tunnels under the Baths, but be sure to book in advance because the tours fill up quickly.

A quick note on the order of the books in this series. The novella *Menace at the Christmas Market* actually comes after this book, even though it was released before *Death in an Elegant City*. So chronologically, *Menace* is number five in the series while *Elegant City* is book number four. I had intended for *Death in an Elegant City* to come after the novella, but books often don't behave as I expect them to when I'm writing them.

Thanks again for spending time with Kate and Alex. They will encounter more mysteries soon so sign up for my newsletter to stay informed of new releases, and, as always, I really appreciate your on-line reviews. I hope *Death in an Elegant City* has given you a fun escape from your everyday life and provided a good puzzle along the way. :)

ABOUT THE AUTHOR

USA Today bestselling author Sara Rosett writes fun mysteries. Her books are light-hearted escapes for readers who enjoy interesting settings, quirky characters, and puzzling mysteries. *Publishers Weekly* called Sara's books, "satisfying," "well-executed," and "sparkling."

Sara loves to get new stamps in her passport and considers dark chocolate a daily requirement. Find out more at Sara-Rosett.com.

Connect with Sara
www.SaraRosett.com

OTHER BOOKS BY SARA ROSETT

This is Sara Rosett's complete library at the time of publication, but Sara has new books coming out all the time. Sign up for her newsletter to stay up to date on new releases.

Murder on Location — English village cozy mysteries

Death in the English Countryside

Death in an English Cottage

Death in a Stately Home

Death in an Elegant City

Menace at the Christmas Market (novella)

Death in an English Garden

Death at an English Wedding

High Society Lady Detective — 1920s country house mysteries

Murder at Archly Manor

Murder at Blackburn Hall

The Egyptian Antiquities Murder

Murder in Black Tie

An Old Money Murder in Mayfair

Murder on a Midnight Clear

Murder at the Mansions

On the Run — Travel, intrigue, and a dash of romance

Elusive

Secretive

Deceptive

Suspicious

Devious

Treacherous

Duplicity

Ellie Avery — Mom-lit cozy mysteries

Moving is Murder

Staying Home is a Killer

Getting Away is Deadly

Magnolias, Moonlight, and Murder

Mint Juleps, Mayhem, and Murder

Mimosas, Mischief, and Murder

Mistletoe, Merriment and Murder

Milkshakes, Mermaids, and Murder

Marriage, Monsters-in-law, and Murder

Mother's Day, Muffins, and Murder

Made in the USA
Monee, IL
19 June 2023

36219545R00152